The message ~~was~~
blatantly clea~~r~~

Shelby began to quiver in anticipation. Embarrassed by how shaky she felt, she put both hands behind her back and leaned against the wall, pretending to be casual but desperately needing the support.

"Shelby." Boone's voice was strained. "Don't lean like that." His gaze lingered on her breasts, and his breathing grew ragged.

She realized that her attempt to be casual had resulted in her breasts thrusting out in what looked like an invitation. She hadn't done it deliberately, but as she noticed his agitation— and the evidence of his arousal—her nervousness began to disappear.

And she discovered something very wicked about herself. Now that he'd said he wasn't in love with someone else, she was ready to play on his weakness for her.

"Tell me to go away, Shelby." His attention became fixed on her mouth. "For God's sake, don't look so ready to be kissed. You're driving me crazy, you know that."

"I know." Meeting the challenge in his eyes, she moistened her lips and parted them, teasing him with a sultry look. "Drive me crazy, too, Boone. Just one last time...."

Dear Reader,

Willie Nelson tells us that mamas shouldn't let their babies grow up to be cowboys. I suppose he's entitled to his opinion. Personally, I wouldn't look forward to a world without cowboys, which is where Willie's advice might take us. I think I could round up a number of women who would agree with me.

Take Boone Connor. (And I'm sure plenty of us would love to.) Six feet five inches of lean, muscular cowboy. Boone's a perfect example of why Willie should rethink his position. I'm extremely grateful Boone's mama let him grow up to be a cowboy. Dressing that yummy man in a business suit would be a crying shame.

As my miniseries THREE COWBOYS & A BABY continues, Boone is daddy prospect number three. Like Sebastian (in #780 *The Colorado Kid*) and Travis (in #784 *Two in the Saddle*), Boone's positive he's baby Elizabeth's father. But is he? Watch for the conclusion of the series when *That's My Baby!*, a Harlequin single-title release, comes out in September. One thing you can count on: Elizabeth's daddy will turn out to be...a cowboy!

Warmly,

Vicki Lewis Thompson

Vicki Lewis Thompson
BOONE'S BOUNTY

HARLEQUIN®

TORONTO • NEW YORK • LONDON
AMSTERDAM • PARIS • SYDNEY • HAMBURG
STOCKHOLM • ATHENS • TOKYO • MILAN • MADRID
PRAGUE • WARSAW • BUDAPEST • AUCKLAND

To the Goddesses of the Temptation e-mail loop,
who coached me on the care and feeding
of three-year-olds. You're the best!

ISBN 0-373-25888-7

BOONE'S BOUNTY

Copyright © 2000 by Vicki Lewis Thompson.

Visit us at www.eHarlequin.com

Printed in U.S.A.

1

Snow.

Boone Connor sighed and switched on the wipers. Didn't it just figure he'd hit a late-season snowstorm on his way over Raton Pass. Damn. It was nearly June. The snow should be gone by now. But his luck had been running that way lately.

And this didn't promise to be one of those wimpy storms that sifted down from the clouds like cake flour and dusted the pine trees so they looked like a Christmas card. This wasn't the kind of snow that blew off the road like white sand. Nope. This was a serious, drifts-to-your-crotch, black-ice-on-the-curves kind of storm. His truck tires were already losing traction.

The roadblock didn't surprise him, but it sure frustrated the hell out of him. His old king-cab could make it through anything, and he sure was anxious about getting to the Rocking D to see that baby. *His* baby, most likely. The idea that he probably had a kid still made him dizzy. He couldn't quite believe the baby was real, and setting eyes on her would help anchor his thoughts.

But Smoky was about to throw a crimp in his plans, obviously.

Boone rolled down his window and snow blew in, nipping his cheeks with cold. He ignored the discomfort and tipped up the brim of his Stetson so he could look the cop in the eye while he tried to make a case for getting past those orange and white barriers.

The patrolman, bundled to the teeth, looked up at Boone. "I'm afraid you'll have to turn back, sir." His breath fogged the air. "Road conditions are bad up ahead and getting worse by the minute."

"My truck's gots four-wheel drive, Officer," Boone said, although he didn't expect that information to make any difference. "And I've driven this road hundreds of times. I need to get to Colorado right away."

"I understand that, sir." The patrolman didn't sound particularly understanding. He sounded as if he was sick to death of standing in the cold reciting this speech to unhappy folks. "But we can't let you take a chance on that road until the storm's over and the snowplow clears it. With luck we'll be able to let people through tomorrow morning."

"Hell."

"There's a little motel and café about three miles back," the patrolman added, stomping his booted feet.

Boone knew the place. He'd stopped there for coffee a few times, but hadn't bothered this trip because he'd been trying to outrun the snow. He'd never stayed at the motel. He mostly liked driving straight through until he got to where he was going. The motel wasn't very big, as he recalled. Ten or twelve units, maybe.

He glanced up at the patrolman. "How many people have you sent there?"

"A few. But I expect most of them drove on back to Santa Fe. The motel's clean, but not exactly the Plaza." The patrolman glanced past Boone's truck. "I'll have to ask you to move your vehicle, sir. There's someone behind you."

Boone glanced in his rearview mirror and saw the small white sedan, its fog lights picking out the flakes and causing them to sparkle while the rest of the car was nearly invisible

in the swirling snow. Now *that* vehicle had no business trying to maneuver down the road ahead, but Boone still
thought he could make it with no sweat. Still, he knew a losing battle when he saw one. He put the truck in gear and
swung it around to the other lane.

As he paused to roll up his window, he glanced over at
the sedan. Its window slid down, and he caught a quick
glimpse of the driver—young, blond and female. With her
hair caught up in a funky ponytail on top of her head, she
looked even younger than she probably was. His irritation
with Smoky eased a little as he considered how vulnerable
that woman would have been if no one had set up a roadblock to protect her from doing something stupid.

He heard her arguing hotly with the officer, and he shook
his head in amazement. Yep, without that roadblock, she'd
have done something real stupid. She'd have ended up a
statistic for sure, off in a snowbank, frozen solid.

He rolled up his window and headed back down toward
the motel, still marveling at how naive that woman was,
thinking she'd drive that little bitty compact over a snow-
choked mountain pass. Better to have the roadblock, even if
it meant he'd get delayed, than to leave greenhorns like that
free to take chances with their lives.

WHEN SHELBY MCFARLAND first saw the roadblock, she pan-
icked, sure that Mason Fowler had reported her to the police. But no, the barricades were on account of the weather.
The patrolman wanted her to turn back.

But turning back meant possibly heading toward Mason,
who by now could be in hot pursuit. She abandoned her
usual caution.

"You don't understand," she said to the officer standing
beside the car. "I *must* get through. The road can't be that
bad!"

"I'm afraid it is, ma'am. You wouldn't stand a chance with this light vehicle." He leaned down and looked into the car. "And I'm sure you wouldn't want to take any risks with that little guy. You a Spurs fan, son?"

"Yep," Josh replied. "Bob, he is, too."

Shelby glanced over at Josh sitting in his car seat, proudly wearing his San Antonio Spurs jersey. She should have dressed him in something less identifiable, but he loved that jersey. And of course, she couldn't risk ending up marooned in a snowbank, not with Josh in the car. What had she been thinking?

Josh stared in fascination at the patrolman. "Do you gots a gun?" he asked.

"Yes, son, I do," the officer said solemnly.

"My daddy gots a gun," Josh said.

Shelby felt sick to her stomach. She didn't doubt Mason had a gun, but the thought of Josh somehow coming into contact with it scared the daylights out of her. "How do you know that, sweetheart?"

"He showed me it."

Shelby closed her eyes briefly, as if that would block out the ugly image. If she needed any more reasons to keep this child away from Mason, there was a huge one. A gun and a three-year-old. She shuddered.

"I hope your daddy keeps that gun locked up good and tight," the patrolman said. "Guns are not toys."

"The policeman is absolutely right, Josh," Shelby said. "You must never touch a gun." And if she had anything to do with it, he'd never get the chance again. She glanced back at the officer. "I want to thank you for preventing me from doing something foolish. I wasn't thinking clearly a moment ago. Trying to go over that pass tonight would be suicide."

"Bob and me, we never seed any snow before," Josh offered.

The patrolman peered into the car. "You got a little dog in there named Bob?"

"No," Shelby said. "Bob is Josh's special friend, and he's very talented. He can make himself invisible."

"Ahhh." The patrolman nodded solemnly. Then he glanced at Shelby. "There's a motel and café back down the road about three miles. Maybe you could wait it out there."

Shelby didn't remember the place, but it sounded better than driving to Santa Fe. "How long will it be before the road's open, do you think?"

"Hard to say, ma'am. If I was you, I'd try to get a room for the night. They're not fancy, but they're clean."

Shelby took a shaky breath. She didn't know for sure that Mason was following her, but she had a bad feeling he was. All he would have had to do was ask her apartment manager where she'd gone. The manager had been on his way into the building just as she and Josh were leaving, and Josh had blurted out that they were going to Yellowstone to ride horsies. She hadn't remembered to tell Josh it was a secret.

Still, she had a head start on Mason, so the motel was probably a safe bet for tonight. Besides, it wasn't as if she had a lot of choice. "Okay," she said. "We'll try that. And thanks again."

"No problem. Just doing my job, ma'am. 'Bye, son."

"'Bye, Mister Policeman."

Shelby gave the officer a smile before rolling up the window. Then she waited for him to step aside before she guided the car around in a half circle. Fortunately no one else seemed to be coming up the road.

Three days ago—it seemed like three years—Mason had called to say he was coming over the next morning to take Josh to the zoo. Something about the arrogant way he'd announced his intentions instead of asking Shelby if that was okay put her on alert. He'd been dropping hints for weeks that if the courts didn't grant him custody, he'd take Josh anyway.

The longer she thought about his brusque tone during the call, the more she became convinced that Mason didn't intend to bring Josh back. So she'd rented a car, hoping that would throw Mason off a little, packed some clothes for her and Josh, and left town.

"Where're we goin', Shebby?" Josh asked. "Back home?"

"No, not home, Josh. But we can't keep going up the mountain road because there's too much snow. So we'll stay overnight in a motel and try again tomorrow morning, okay?"

"Okay, but when are we gonna get to Yellowstone? You *said*, Shebby. Bob wants to see geezers."

"*Geysers*, Josh."

"Yeah, those. And we're gonna ride horsies there, right?"

"That's the plan." She should change the plan, but Josh was so excited she didn't have the heart, at least not yet.

"Bob, he knows how to ride horsies real good. He's gonna teach me."

"Good thing Bob knows so much, huh?" Shelby said. Right about now she wished Josh's imaginary friend really existed, and that he was about six-five, weighed two-fifty and could bench-press his own weight.

"Bob, he knows *this* much." Josh spread his arms wide. "A whole bunch, is what Bob knows." He glanced at Shelby, as if he expected her to contradict him. "Right, Shebby?"

Shelby smiled. No matter how scary life got, she took heart from this little bundle of sunshine sitting in his car seat next to her. He was unsinkable. And so damned normal, with his love of basketball and his imaginary friend. A child psychologist might say the imaginary friend had made an appearance at this particular time because of what Josh had been through recently. That could be true, and if so, she was impressed with the way the little boy took care of his own needs.

She glanced over at Josh. "Right. Bob is awesome."

Josh nodded. "Awesome. When are we gonna see geezers?"

"Well, first we have to go all the way through Colorado, and then most of the way through Wyoming. But before we do that, we have to get over this mountain, and we can't do that until tomorrow morning."

"'Member that song about a mountain? The one we singed in school?"

"Sure. Want to sing it?"

"Yep." Josh launched into a close approximation of "She'll Be Comin' 'Round the Mountain."

Shelby joined in, helping him through the parts he'd forgotten. How she loved this little boy. Long ago, in spite of herself, she'd begun to think of him as her own child. He even looked like her—same blond hair, same blue eyes. Patricia hadn't ever seemed to have time for him, especially after she'd divorced Mason.

And during the breakup of Patricia's marriage, Shelby's parents had been so busy worrying about Patricia, their favorite child, that they hadn't seemed to have any concern left for Josh. And now all three of them were gone—her sister and both her parents.

Shelby's chest tightened as a nick of pain touched her heart, like the whisper of a very sharp knife that barely cuts the skin but is capable of dealing a killing blow. It was a warning sign that she needed to shut down her emotions, and fast. Ever since the boating accident four months ago that had claimed her parents and Patricia, Shelby had kept a tight rein on her feelings. She had Josh to think about.

Josh stopped singing as Shelby pulled into the parking lot of a small motel with a café nearby.

"Is this it?" he asked.

"This is it." Shelby surveyed the rambling building, which was in definite need of a paint job. Her parents would have turned up their noses at the accommodations, but Shelby was grateful for anything reasonably clean. Quite a few cars and trucks were gathered in the lot, and she hoped she wouldn't have any trouble getting a room.

And she definitely wanted one. Driving all the way back to Santa Fe was too risky. The lights shining through the café's windows made it look cozy in the gathering gloom brought on by the heavy snowfall. The thought of a hot cup of coffee beckoned to her, but she turned the wheel left and parked in front of the first unit of the motel where an orange neon sign in one corner of the window read Office. In the opposite corner was another neon sign in blue that said Vacancy.

Shelby sighed with relief.

"They don't gots no swimmin' pool," Josh said. "Bob was gonna go swimmin'."

Shelby laughed as she unbuckled her seat belt and reached in the back for their coats and hats. "Bob must be a member of the Polar Bear Club."

"Huh?" Josh giggled. "Bob's not a *bear*."

"The Polar Bear Club is a bunch of people who go swimming when it's really cold outside." Shelby helped him get out of the car seat and into his coat and hat. "So they call themselves Polar Bears."

"Do they gots white fur?"

"No, they wear bathing suits." She zipped up his jacket and decided she didn't need to fasten the chin strap on his hat for the quick trip inside. "Just like you do when you go swimming. Now stay right there, and I'll come around and get you out. If I carry you in, I won't have to bother putting your boots on."

"I can walk, y'know. I'm a big boy."

"I know." Shelby put on her own coat. "But the snow's started to drift out there."

"Bob wants to play in it."

"We'll see." But she knew she couldn't allow Josh to play out in the snow in front of the motel. He'd be way too visible.

As she started to get out of the car, the sign in the window changed to No Vacancy. "Oh, no!"

"What, Shebby?"

"Uh, nothing, Josh. Sit tight. I'll be right there to get you." Grabbing her purse, she stepped into the snow, ignoring the icy dampness soaking her running shoes as she closed the car door and ran around to get Josh. She'd talk the motel owner into letting her spend the night somewhere in this building, even if it was on a cot in a broom closet. She'd sit up all night and let Josh have a mattress on the floor, if necessary. But they couldn't spend the night in the café, where Mason could come along and find them.

She slung the shoulder strap of her purse bandolier-style across her body before lifting Josh out of the car.

He turned his face up to the snow and laughed with delight. "It tickles!"

"I guess it does, at that." She hurried toward the office door.

"It tastes like Popsicles! I gots some on my tongue! See?"

"Oh, sweetheart, I can't right now. I will. Later I will." She hated not being able to enjoy Josh's first experience with snow. She hated this whole mess, in fact. A bolt of pure anger shot through her. Damn them, all of them, for not putting this little boy first in their lives. Damn them for taking her dad's high-speed boat out on such a foggy day. Damn them all for dying. Now Josh had no one but her. Somehow, she would have to be enough.

A buzzer sounded when she opened the office door. She hurried inside, adding her wet tracks to the ones already covering the carpet. A very tall cowboy stood at the scarred counter, his back to her while he filled out a registration form. He looked at least seven feet tall, but Shelby guessed part of that was due to the heels of his boots and the crown of his hat.

The desk clerk, an older man with glasses, peered around the cowboy. "I'm really sorry, but I just rented our last room." He pointed to the No Vacancy sign in the window. "We're full up."

"Surely there's somewhere you can put us," Shelby said. "I only need a cot for Josh. I can take the floor. We're desperate."

The cowboy laid down the pen he'd been using and turned to look at her.

The sheer size of him made her take an involuntary step back. Then she looked into his eyes, which were an incredible shade of green. But more than that, they were the kindest eyes she'd ever seen. Although she had no logical reason to feel better, she did.

"You forgot Bob." Josh clapped his cold hands against her cheeks and forced her head around so she had to look at him. "Bob, he needs someplace to sleep, y'know," Josh explained, his blue eyes earnest. He looked so cute, with his hat on crooked and the chin strap dangling down.

"I know," she whispered, giving him a quick kiss on the cheek.

"Well, that makes it really hard," the clerk said. "Even if I could figure out something, I'm afraid we don't allow pets."

"The dog'll probably be okay in the car for the night," the

big cowboy said quietly. "You and the boy can take my room."

Shelby realized how close to the surface her emotions were when the offer made tears gather in her eyes. "Oh, I couldn't —"

"Bob, he's not a dog," Josh said. "He's my friend."

The cowboy frowned. "You left another kid out in the car? It's mighty cold out there for a—"

"No, it's not another kid," Shelby said. "Bob is—"

"Awesome!" Josh said.

"Yes, he is," Shelby said as she looked the cowboy in the eye and hoped he would get the message as quickly as the patrolman had. "He's so awesome that he can make himself invisible if he wants to." She lowered Josh to the floor and took off his hat. "As a matter of fact, Josh, I happen to know he can sleep anywhere, because he told me so. He could even sleep *under* your bed if he wanted to, and be perfectly comfy."

Josh's forehead crinkled in thought. "You're sure?"

"It's one of his special tricks." She glanced over at the cowboy to see if he was buying the story.

He was. His smile was gentle as he inclined his head just the faintest bit in her direction, letting her know he had Bob all figured out.

That soft, understanding smile made her insides quiver a little, reminding her of pleasures she hadn't enjoyed in quite a while. And it would be a while longer, considering how her life was going these days.

"Then it's settled," the cowboy said. "You, the boy and...Bob can have unit six."

"But what about you?" She desperately wanted the room, but she felt guilty taking him up on his offer.

"No problem."

She gazed into his ruggedly handsome face. If they were

in a movie, she'd suggest sharing the room, platonically, of course. Her tummy quivered again. But this was no movie. She turned to the clerk. "Is there anything else? Maybe a large closet, or—"

"I'll be fine," the cowboy said. "Don't worry about a thing. The café's open twenty-four hours. I'll just stretch out in a booth and make myself at home."

"But—"

"Hey. I'm used to such things. If the weather wasn't so nasty, I wouldn't have even bothered with a motel. I'd have slept in my truck, which I've done a million times. So it's no big deal for me." His gaze rested on Josh. "I want to make sure that little cowpoke gets his rest."

Shelby's heart swelled with gratitude. Right when she needed a knight in shining armor, one had appeared. "I can't thank you enough," she said, her voice husky from the lump in her throat. And those damn pesky tears kept trying to well up in her eyes. She blinked them back. "You're a very nice man."

"Don't mention it." With a touch of his fingers to the brim of his hat, he walked past her out into the snow, leaving behind the scent of leather and denim.

"What a gentleman," she said, thinking how well it fit the tall cowboy. He was truly a *gentle man.*

"He is, at that," the clerk said. He was gazing after the cowboy with an expression of great respect. "Those booths are made of molded plastic. I'd hate to spend the night in one."

"I'll have to find a way to repay him," Shelby said as she fished in her purse for her wallet and took out her credit card. Belatedly she thought to glance at the registration form the cowboy had left on the counter. She caught the name Boone Connor printed boldly across the top line be-

fore the desk clerk whisked the form away and crumpled it
up.

Boone. She smiled. What a perfect name for him. He'd definitely been a boon to her, that was for sure.

Josh tugged on the leg of her jeans. "Can Bob and me read
those? They gots horsies."

Shelby glanced to where Josh pointed and saw some
western magazines on a table. She looked up at the clerk. "Is
it okay? He knows not to tear pages out or anything."

"Sure, it's okay." The desk clerk smiled down at Josh.
"Go ahead and read the magazines, son."

Shelby watched Josh go over to the table, carefully choose
a magazine, and climb up in a ratty overstuffed chair before
he started slowly turning the pages and muttering to himself, pretending he was reading. Every once in a while he
glanced beside him and pointed out something in the magazine. Obviously he was sharing the experience with Bob.

"He's a fine boy," the clerk said. "You must be a proud
momma."

"Oh, I—" Shelby caught herself before she told the clerk
she was not Josh's mother. It was an automatic response,
one she'd become used to giving because she'd taken care of
Josh so much.

She'd once calculated that she'd spent more time with
him than Patricia had. That had turned out to be a blessing,
all things considered. If Josh had been closer to his mother
and his grandparents, he would have been more grief-
stricken when they had disappeared from his life. As it was,
he seemed sad and definitely a little confused, but not over-
whelmed.

Shelby was obviously the most important person in his
world, but now was not the time to advertise the fact that
Josh was her nephew, not her son. And besides, some day

she hoped to be his mother, legally. If only Patricia had left a will, that wouldn't be so damned complicated, either.

She brushed the thoughts away and smiled at the clerk. "I am very proud of Josh," she said.

2

ALL SIX BOOTHS in the small café were full, but Boone had expected that. Later on, as people returned to their rooms, the place would empty out. Then he'd stake out a booth for the night.

He'd forgotten the bench seats were the hard plastic kind. Oh, well. He would have done the same thing, even if he'd remembered. He would have done the same thing if the seats had been made of barbed wire. A woman with a little kid needed a motel room more than he did. *A pretty woman.* He pushed the thought aside. He wasn't in the market for a pretty woman.

Taking a stool at the counter, he ordered a cup of coffee from the café's only waitress. Her name was Lucy according to the tag she wore, and she was definitely pregnant. She also looked worn-out, probably from handling a bigger crowd than usual.

"You live around here, Lucy?" he asked her as she poured him some coffee.

"Not too far away." She moved with precision that came from experience. "Why?"

Boone glanced out the window before looking back at her. "The way it's coming down out there, seems like you ought to head home while you still can."

She gave him a weary smile. "That's right nice of you to think of that. As a matter of fact, I am leaving in about another hour, after we get these folks fed. The couple who owns this place said they could handle everything. No need for Mr. Sloan to hang around the motel office now that the rooms are all rented, so he's gonna come over here and help Mrs. Sloan so I can leave."

Boone nodded. "Good. You got four-wheel drive?"

"Yeah. My hubby's coming to pick me up in the Jeep." She looked down shyly at her belly. "He's sort of protective these days."

"He should be," Boone said.

Her cheeks turned a happy shade of pink. "I'm hoping for a boy, but Gary doesn't care what we have, so long as the baby's healthy. I—" She paused and broke eye contact as someone in a booth called her name. "Excuse me. Table two needs some looking after." She bustled out from behind the counter and hurried over to the booth in question.

Boone had the urge to take over for her so she could put her feet up until her husband arrived. Sure, some activity was good for a woman in her condition, but not this much. He'd make a damn poor waitress, though, and he doubted she'd let him help her, anyway. Leastways not after he'd broken a few dishes and mixed up a couple of orders.

So he sipped his coffee and thought about whether Jessica had worked too hard while she was pregnant with Elizabeth. She should have notified him right away when she found out she was pregnant. Thinking of her struggling through the pregnancy and birth by herself drove him crazy with guilt.

The coffee had warmed him up considerably, so he took off his leather jacket and laid it across his lap. Then he unsnapped the breast pocket of his shirt and took out the note he'd gotten from Jessica. He'd read it about a million times, yet he still needed to keep looking at it to convince himself this wasn't some bad dream he was having.

Dear Boone,

I'm counting on you to be a godfather to Elizabeth until I can return for her. Your quiet strength is just what she needs right now. I've left her with Sebastian at the Rocking D. Believe me, I wouldn't do this if I weren't in desperate circumstances.

In deepest gratitude, Jessica

The letter was dated more than two months ago. She'd gotten the zip code wrong, so that had delayed it some, and then when it had finally arrived in Las Cruces, he'd been on the road hunting up horseshoeing jobs.

Still holding the letter, Boone rubbed his chin and gazed out the window at the steady snow. Snow had landed him in this fix in the first place. More than two years ago he'd let his three best buddies—Sebastian Daniels, Travis Evans and Nat Grady—talk him into a skiing trip in Aspen. He didn't belong on skis any more than a buffalo belonged on roller skates, but he'd gone for Sebastian's sake. They'd all nearly gotten themselves killed in an avalanche while they were blundering around on the slopes.

Jessica Franklin had been working the front desk of the ski lodge, and it was their dumb luck that they'd struck up a friendship with her and she'd offered to go with them that day. Otherwise Nat would've been toast. Jessica had figured out where he was buried and had kept her head, directing the rest of them to help dig him out before he smothered.

"More coffee?" Lucy asked as she passed by again.

Boone glanced at his cup. It would be a long night, and he could probably use the caffeine. "Sure," he said, smiling at her. "And thanks."

"Anytime."

After she left, he resumed staring out the window, and his thoughts returned to his predicament. He wished he could think about something else, but he couldn't. If only he hadn't gone to the avalanche reunion party last year. He'd thought the idea was kind of morbid, but once again he'd gone along with the crowd.

Besides, he'd needed the distraction. Darlene had just announced that she was breaking up with him to marry that dork Chester Littlefield.

As it had turned out, Nat hadn't made it to the reunion party because of some prior commitment. That had left Boone, Jessica, Sebastian and Travis to celebrate. Boone didn't usually drink much. Over the years he'd seen what liquor could do to a man while watching his father's bouts with the bottle.

But that night, thinking about Darlene, he'd guzzled everything in sight. Sebastian and Travis had put away a fair amount themselves, but Jessica, being a good friend, had stayed sober so she could drive them back to their cabin and see that they all took some aspirin before they tumbled into bed.

And that was when Boone figured he'd stepped over the line and dragged Jessica into bed with him. Sober he'd never have considered such a thing. But drunk and depressed about Darlene, he might well have.

He was sure Jessica knew he hadn't meant to, that he didn't think of her like that. Hell, he'd probably called her Darlene in the middle of it all. So Jessica had shouldered the whole burden when she found out she was pregnant. But now she was in some kind of trouble and had asked him to be a "godfather."

Boone didn't buy that godfather label, not for a minute. He was the baby's father. When he'd called the Rocking D, he'd found out that Sebastian and Travis had gotten letters naming them as godfathers, too. But those other letters were a smokescreen. Sebastian was too honorable to have done such a thing, and Travis was too experienced to be caught like that. Besides, Jessica easily could have shoved those two guys away, considering they were drunk.

But even drunk, Boone had the strength of two men. Jessica wouldn't have been able to get away. He hoped to hell he hadn't hurt her. He'd spend the rest of his life trying to make it up to her for being a brute. And he would never touch another drop of alcohol as long as he lived.

"Mr. Connor?"

The soft voice brought him back to his surroundings. Turning from the window, he realized the blonde and her little boy were standing right next to him. Quickly he folded Jessica's letter, tucked it in his pocket and snapped the pocket closed. Then he stood.

"Sorry," the woman said. "You don't have to get up. I didn't mean to disturb you."

"No problem," he said. Women were constantly surprised by his manners, but he couldn't help that. His mother had taught him to stand in the presence of a lady, and he couldn't change that training now, even if he'd wanted to. "How did you know my name?"

Color tinged her cheeks. "I looked at the registration form before the clerk threw it away." She held out her hand. "My name is Shelby McFarland."

"Pleased to meet you, Shelby." He took her soft hand gently in his, careful not to put too much pressure into his handshake. She was so delicate, he imagined he could leave a bruise if he was the least bit enthusiastic.

He enjoyed the contact, though, enjoyed it more than was good for him. He liked looking into her blue eyes, too. He read basic goodness and honesty there, but she was wary, too, as if something was spooking her. He put that together with the way she'd argued with the Smoky about going up

the hill and wondered if she was running from something...or someone.

"And this is Josh," she said, bringing the little boy forward. "Josh, can you shake Mr. Connor's hand?"

Josh nodded and stuck out his hand, but his eyes widened
as he looked Boone up and down. "You're big as a *elephant*,"
he said.

"Josh!" Shelby reddened.

Boone laughed out loud. "Can't argue with the truth, son.
I'm about as graceful as one, too." He glanced around. "I'm
afraid all the booths are taken up, so if you're here to eat,
you'll have to grab a couple of stools." The prospect of having her sit down beside him gave him a forbidden thrill.
Then he thought of the note in his pocket and reminded
himself of his reason for being on this road in the first place.

"Oh, we're not staying," she said.

He frowned. Surely she wasn't going back out in that
snowstorm now that she had a roof over her head. And
truth be told, he didn't appreciate having his generosity
thrown back in his face.

She must have figured out he was ticked, because she put
her hand lightly on his arm. "I mean we're not staying in the
café," she said quickly. "We'll just get something to go.
We're definitely staying in the room you so graciously gave
up. That's what I wanted to talk to you about. I would like to
do...something in return. Buying your dinner seems inadequate, but I can at least do that much."

Her touch on his arm felt like the nuzzle of a timid foal.
And now that he looked closer, he could see that her whole
body was poised for flight. She'd glanced over at the door
several times. His curiosity grew.

"How 'bout a star?" Josh asked. "When I'm a good boy,
like when I 'membered to pick up my room, you give'd me
a star."

Shelby blushed. "Well, that's a good idea, Josh, but I'm not sure that Mr. Connor—"

"The name's Boone, and I'd love a star." He probably shouldn't have said that. No doubt about it, he was having trouble keeping his distance from these two.

"Uh, okay." She looked flustered, but she dug around in her purse and came up with a sheet of peel-and-stick gold stars. She peeled one off. "Where...where do you want it?"

Even if he was creating a problem for himself, he couldn't help loving this. "On my shirt's fine."

She looked him over, and finally stuck the star on the flap of his shirt pocket, smoothing it carefully without looking at him. Her cheeks were bright pink. "There," she said, glancing up. "There's your star."

"And a kiss!" Josh said.

Boone knew he should tell her to forget the kiss, but he couldn't make himself say it. Only a fool would turn down a kiss from someone as adorable as Shelby, with her ponytail perched on her head and that sweet blush on her cheeks.

"A star and a kiss!" Josh insisted. "You *always* do that."

Apparently she decided that giving in quickly was better than making a bigger scene by protesting. Standing on tiptoe, she leaned over and gave Boone a quick peck on the cheek.

Her lips were soft and full, and her scent swirled around him. He fought the urge to close his eyes with pleasure. But he needed to keep the moment light, so he grinned at her. "Thanks. Now I've been fully rewarded."

"I do appreciate the room," she said shyly.

"You're most welcome. Listen why not stay and eat here? Taking the food back to the room will be a real hassle in this weather." Well, hell. He seemed determined to dig himself into a hole. If he didn't watch it, he'd ask for her phone number next.

Fortunately for both of them, she didn't fall in with his plan. A wary look flashed in her eyes again, and she glanced away. Boone had the strangest feeling she was thinking of some story to explain why she couldn't stay in the café to eat dinner.

"Bob wants to stay," Josh said. "'Cause Bob gots to go potty."

Shelby looked down at him. "I'm sure it won't take long for them to whip up a couple of burgers and fries. Can Bob wait until we go back to the room?"

Josh held his crotch and peered up at her. "I gots to go, too," he whispered. "Real bad, Shebby."

Shebby. Boone heard it, plain as day. No way had the kid said *Mommy* just then. Shebby was probably his version of her name, Shelby. This wasn't her son. The word *kidnapper* flashed in his brain, but he just couldn't buy it.

She sighed and looked around until she located the sign for the rest rooms. "Okay." She glanced up at Boone. "If you'll excuse us, we'll—"

"Do I hafta go in where the ladies go?" Josh hung back, his gaze pleading.

"Yes." She took his hand firmly in hers.

Josh hung on her hand and tried to plant his feet. "But last time that lady was laughin' at me."

"She was laughing at the Cheerios, Josh, not at you. We don't have to use them this time if you don't want to. Now come on."

Boone had to ask. "Cheerios?"

Shelby glanced back at him. "I throw some in the bowl. It gives him a target."

Josh gazed up at Boone with a worried expression, as if he now expected Boone to laugh, too.

Boone bit down on the inside of his lip so he wouldn't.

"Great idea," he said, although his voice was husky with the laugh he'd swallowed.

Josh's expression cleared and his smile came out like sunshine. He pointed a stubby finger at Boone. "Me and him could go."

Shelby shook her head and tugged on his hand. "No, I'm afraid not, Josh. Now come on."

"*Please*," Josh wailed, hanging back and dragging his feet. "I wanna be a big boy."

Boone's heart went out to him. He remembered a few trips to the ladies' room, himself, when he was a kid. He'd always been tall for his age, so a couple of women had given him the evil eye when his mother had insisted on taking him in with her. He'd hated every minute of it, although now he completely understood why she'd done that. The world had some sick people in it.

"I'd be glad to take him," Boone said. "I realize you don't really know me, but—"

"I know you," Josh said. "You gave us a room. Please, Shebby. Let me and him go."

Shelby paused. She looked exhausted, frustrated and scared. "Okay," she said at last. "If you're willing to do that, I appreciate it. While you're gone I'll put in our order. Can I get anything for you while I'm at it? I'd love to be able to buy you some dinner."

"No, thanks." Boone had decided that eating would be his main entertainment tonight, and he didn't want to rush it. "I'm not really hungry yet."

She seemed even more frustrated that she couldn't repay him with dinner, but Josh began hopping up and down, so she put the boy's hand in Boone's. "Thank you for everything," she said. "You've been a real godsend."

"Glad to help." He touched a hand to the brim of his hat, which coaxed a faint smile from her. Then he had to focus all his attention on keeping Josh's tiny hand in his. Such a small hand. Boone had to lean to the right to keep hold of it as Josh ran along beside him on the way to the rest rooms.

"Do you gots horsies?" Josh sounded breathless but determined to communicate. "'Cause me and Bob, we like horsies. We're gonna ride some in Yellowstone."

Boone realized the little guy was puffing because Boone's stride was too long. He shortened it. "I have two horses," he said. "One I keep with my friend Sebastian at the Rocking D, and the other one I keep at my folks' place in Las Cruces."

"Rocking D? What's a Rocking D?"

Boone pushed open the swinging door to the rest room. "A ranch."

"A *ranch*? You gots a *ranch*, like on TV?" Josh seemed beside himself with excitement, so beside himself that he'd obviously forgotten why he was in the rest room in the first place.

"Well, it's not my—"

"Can I come there? Can I?"

"We'll talk about that later. Right now you'd better tend to business."

"'Kay." Josh headed for a stall.

"You can do it here if you want," Boone said as he gestured toward a urinal. "I'll hold you up."

Josh turned back to him, his expression confused.

"Come on. I'll show you. This is how big guys do it." Boone demonstrated.

Josh watched in obvious fascination.

Boone zipped up and glanced over at Josh. "Ready to try?"

Josh nodded vigorously.

In the end, Boone decided it would work best if he crouched down and let Josh stand on his knees. The little boy chortled happily all through the process, as if it was the highlight of his day.

Boone realized he was having a great time. What fun it would be to show a kid like this around the Rocking D. Sebastian had that gentle gelding, Samson, who would be perfect for Josh to learn on. But that was a pipe dream, for sure. Boone didn't think Shelby would make a special detour to the Rocking D. She looked like a lady on a mission.

Besides, Boone had no business daydreaming about taking her there. She would be too big a temptation. He'd already caught himself thinking about what sort of body was hidden by the bulky ski jacket she wore, and he was in no position to go down that road with any woman.

As Josh finished washing his hands, he started in again on the topic of visiting the ranch. "I never been to a ranch," he said. "Can I come? Me and Bob?"

"I imagine you have places to go and people to see," Boone said.

"Well, we're gonna see geezers in Yellowstone." Josh dropped the paper towel neatly in the waste container.

"You mean geysers?" Boone was impressed with the boy's neatness. Somebody had taught him well.

Josh nodded. "They go whoosh! Up in the air!" He threw his arms up to illustrate.

"Sounds like fun." Boone decided to do some fishing for information. "Are you going to meet your mommy up there?"

"I don't think so. My mommy's in heaven with the angels."

The casual statement slammed into Boone like a brick to the stomach, but Josh seemed completely at ease about it. Shelby probably wasn't a kidnapper, not that Boone had seriously thought she was. But she was nervous about something. "Then maybe your dad?"

"Nope." Josh started marching toward the door of the rest room. "My daddy's in S'Antonio."

"Really?" Boone held the door open for Josh.

"Yep." Josh walked through the door. "He gots a gun."

SHELBY HAD WATCHED Boone lead Josh away and no warning bells had sounded in her head. Boone inspired trust and a sense of security. She could feel it, and she was sure Josh could feel it, too.

Poor little guy hadn't had much in the way of male role models. His grandfather had never been particularly interested in kids, not even his own daughters when they were young. Mason had ignored Josh until he'd smelled money, and even with the lure of that money, Mason had a hard time pretending to be a loving dad.

No wonder Josh had latched on to Boone so quickly. Seeing the way Boone abbreviated his long stride to accommodate Josh's short one made Shelby's heart hitch.

Not all men brushed children aside the way her father had, she reminded herself. Patricia, the beauty, had eventually gained her father's admiration by going into the high-profile world of television broadcasting. He and Shelby's mother had been able to brag about Patricia, who eventually had her own local talk show. Shelby's modest desktop-publishing business and her more average looks hadn't been able to compete.

Shelby watched until Boone led Josh away through the swinging door of the men's room. Then she turned to catch the eye of the waitress working behind the counter. She noticed that her name was Lucy. Shelby's mother's name. Another sharp pain sliced through her before she could shut down her feelings.

The woman, who was visibly pregnant, came over toward Shelby. "Can I help you?"

"You sure can. Can I please get two hamburgers and two orders of fries to go?" Shelby knew it wasn't the most nutritious meal in the world, but she'd worry about getting some green veggies into Josh tomorrow, after they'd put some more miles between them and Mason.

"You and that little boy aren't going back out on the road, are you?" asked the waitress.

"No, thank goodness. We have a room at the motel, thanks to that gentleman who was just sitting here. He had the last room, but he gave it to us, instead."

The waitress's expression grew soft. "Isn't he the nicest man? He was worried about whether I had a way to get home."

"Apparently he's the kind who looks out for others," Shelby said. "It's good to know there are still guys out there like that."

"And he's pretty darned cute, too, did you notice?"

"I guess." Shelby thought about the gentle smile that had made her tingle. Oh, yes, she'd noticed. Besides his understanding green eyes, he also possessed a couple of other noteworthy features, like a very masculine-looking jaw and curly black hair. Her heart had raced when she'd leaned over to place a kiss on his suntanned cheek.

He was built well, too. Although some large men tended to look beefy and slightly out of shape, this one didn't seem to have a spare bit of flab on him. Nice tush, too. Watching him walk away with Josh had given her guilty pleasure.

"It's a wonder some woman hasn't snatched him up," the waitress said. "But he's not wearing a wedding ring. And he's the type who would, if he was married." She glanced pointedly down at the bare ring finger of Shelby's left hand.

Shelby stuffed her left hand into the pocket of her jacket. The waitress might think she could do a little matchmaking in between serving orders, but whether Boone Connor was married or not was of no consequence to Shelby. She couldn't think about such things under the current circumstances. Even ogling his cute tush meant she was allowing herself to be distracted from her goal of keeping Josh safe. That wasn't good.

She leaned closer to the waitress. "Listen, since he'll have to spend the night in the café, could I leave some money with you to pay for whatever food he eats? I'd like to find some way to repay him for being so kind."

"I'll be leaving soon, myself, but I suppose I could arrange that with Mrs. Sloan. Why don't you just stay and eat your dinner when he eats his? Then you could just pick up the check for everything."

Shelby trotted out the excuse she'd been about to give Boone. "Well, I would, but Josh has a program he wants to see on TV, so we need to get back to the room."

The waitress rolled her eyes as if to say that Shelby was crazy to let something like that stand in her way. "If you're sure."

"I'm sure." She pulled some bills out of her purse and gave them to the waitress. "That should cover ours and anything he has, don't you think?"

The waitress looked at the cash Shelby had given her and chuckled. "That's more than enough. I'll go put in your order."

Shelby positioned herself with her back to the counter so she could see the front door of the café. No one had come in for some time, and hardly anyone had left, either. The booths along the wall were still occupied. The place had taken on a party atmosphere, as if being stranded here together had made everyone friends.

Except her. A woman on the run didn't stop to make friends along the way. Too risky. Boone Connor had helped her out, and she was grateful. Under different circumstances, she would have liked to get to know him, but once she left this café tonight, she never expected to see him again.

She'd driven out of San Antonio without much of a plan except an instinctive urge to head for Yellowstone Park. But she couldn't stay in Yellowstone. She'd continue north to Canada.

Once out of the country, she'd find a good lawyer and assess her chances of legally keeping Josh. But she'd keep him, legally or illegally, because she knew one thing for sure. No matter what a judge might say, as long as she was alive Mason Fowler was never, ever getting custody of his son.

3

BOONE HATED TO ADMIT how much he missed Josh and
Shelby once they'd left the café with their bags of food. But
no way would Shelby stay to eat. Something was going on
with her, and Boone was afraid he'd never find out what it
was.

When he learned that she'd left money to pay for his food,
he had half a mind to go over to her room and give it back.
Then he recognized that he was only looking for an excuse
to see her again, which was a fool's errand, for sure. He was
the sort of guy who needed time to build a relationship, and
after tonight, he and Shelby would probably never cross
paths again. That was probably just as well.

Still, he couldn't let Shelby buy his dinner. It didn't seem
right. So he asked Mrs. Sloan to put the money aside for
Lucy, who could probably use some extra cash for that baby
she'd be having soon.

By eleven the café had emptied out and Boone had his
pick of booths, not that one looked any more comfortable
than the other. He was on a first-name basis with Norma
Sloan and her husband Eugene. The couple reminded him
of Jack Sprat who could eat no fat and his wife who could
eat no lean. They'd been more than kind, providing a pillow
and a blanket to help him through the night.

About eleven-thirty, Norma sent Eugene into the café's
back room to grab a catnap while she kept the coffeepot going. Who they were brewing coffee for was a mystery to

Boone, because no other customers showed up. Boone crammed himself into his chosen booth and pulled his hat over his eyes.

When Eugene came out to relieve Norma at one in the morning, Boone unfolded himself from the booth. He didn't think he'd slept much, and he felt as if he'd been rode hard and put away wet. Stretching the stiffness from his spine, he walked over to the counter.

"Want some java, Boone?" Eugene asked around a yawn.

"No, thanks. But why don't you go on back to bed and let me take care of anybody who comes in? I doubt anybody will, anyway."

"That's a nice offer, but my conscience wouldn't let me." Eugene yawned again and poured himself a cup of coffee. "You're a customer, not my hired help."

"Speaking of that, who usually mans the counter when you're open all night? Don't tell me Lucy works graveyard."

"Nope." Eugene unwrapped a sweet roll as he talked. "We have another gal, Edna. She's older than Lucy and says she likes working nights. Prefers the peace and quiet. But I didn't want her on the road tonight, so I called and told her to stay home, that we'd handle it. That's what Norma and I always do when the weather gets like this. We'd rather stay up all night ourselves than worry about an employee skidding all over the road trying to get to work." He bit into the sweet roll. "Want one?"

"No, thanks." Boone turned to gaze out the window at the snow still falling. "Then how about closing the place until morning?" He glanced back at Eugene. "Nobody but a crazy person is still on that road tonight."

Eugene smiled. "No can do. Staying open is a matter of pride with me. My daddy used to own this place, and when I took over he made me promise to keep the coffee going twenty-four hours a day. He said we'd never know how many lives we'd saved by giving people a place to pull off the road, get some coffee and a bite to eat, but he figured we'd saved our share."

"I'll bet you have, at that." Boone rubbed his chin and felt the stubble there. He'd grab a shave in the rest room before he left in the morning. "I've stopped here myself a few times, when I was feeling groggy. You might even have saved me."

"And there could be someone else out there battling his way through the storm, and the light from our sign could be a beacon in the night."

"Like a lighthouse," Boone said. He could understand Eugene's urge to save people. He had that sort of urge all the time. That's why he was sleeping in a booth tonight.

"Exactly," Eugene said. "A lighthouse. You sure you don't want some coffee and one of these rolls?"

Boone sighed. "Yeah, why not. I'm not having much luck sleeping, anyway." And he could tell Eugene wanted somebody to talk to. So he sat at the counter and swapped fishing stories with the guy for a good hour.

He talked so long and grew so tired that sleep sounded like a real possibility, even in a hard plastic booth. But before he could excuse himself from Eugene, the café door opened, bringing with it a blast of frigid air and blowing snow.

Boone swiveled on the stool to see if one of the motel customers had decided to come over for a midnight snack. For one crazy moment he hoped it might even be Shelby. Instead it was someone he didn't recognize from the crowd that had filled the café earlier that night.

The man was built like a fireplug, short but solid. His ski jacket bulked him out even more, but Boone could tell from the fit of the guy's jeans that he probably worked out in some fancy gym to build up his muscles.

"Damn!" The man pulled off a black stocking cap as he stomped his feet on the mat just inside the café door. His hair was cropped close to his head, military-style. "It's a bitch out there!"

Boone usually reserved judgment on folks until they'd had a chance to prove themselves one way or the other, but for some reason this guy put him on edge. There was something hard and unyielding about him that showed in his voice, in his movements, even in the bristle of his haircut.

"I'll bet you could use a cup of coffee," Eugene said eagerly. "And there's some pie left, if you—"

"Black coffee," the man said.

Boone was relieved to see the man order something. For a minute he'd imagined the guy taking out a gun and demanding that Eugene empty the cash register. Staying open all night for weary travelers was one thing, but Boone wondered if Eugene and Norma had ever been left alone to face the wrong kind of customer. This fellow was probably harmless, but all in all Boone was glad to be here tonight, just in case.

"Where're y'all headed?" Boone asked as the guy sat down at the counter. Boone laid on the good-ol'-boy accent on purpose. That, combined with his size, tended to make people think he wasn't very smart, and then he found out things he might not have otherwise.

The man looked Boone over, his pale gray eyes clearly taking Boone's measure. "Nowhere, it appears. Damn storm."

"Yeah, it's holdin' folks up, all right," Boone said.

Eugene set the coffee in front of the man. "Sure I can't get you something to eat? A sandwich?"

"Nothing." The man took a swig of his coffee.

Eugene lifted the pot in Boone's direction and Boone nodded. He didn't need more coffee, but he wanted an excuse to sit at the counter a little longer and find out what this stranger was up to.

"How long before these pansy-ass cops let us through?" the man asked.

Boone decided to play along. "God knows. My truck could make it right now, no sweat, but you know these Smokies. Treat us all like a bunch of old women."

Eugene's eyebrows lifted, and Boone winked at him when the other guy wasn't looking. Eugene grinned and turned to put the coffeepot back on the burner.

"Ain't that the truth," the man muttered. "And then I couldn't rouse anybody at the motel office. Knocked so hard I about broke the door down. Those people must sleep like the dead."

Boone wondered why he'd try to beat down the door of a motel office that had a No Vacancy sign in the window. His sense of uneasiness grew.

Eugene turned to the man. "I'm sorry, but we don't have any rooms left."

"Oh, so you're the one in charge?" The man looked at Eugene with new interest.

"My wife and I run both the motel and the café. All I can offer you is something to eat and drink, and a booth to stretch out in if you like."

"Actually, none of the above." The guy leaned forward. "I want to know if a woman and a little kid checked in after the barricades went up. She's blond, and he's about so high." He held his hand about three feet off the floor.

The pieces clicked into place for Boone. Shelby, arguing with the patrolman. Shelby, desperate for a room. A room to hide in. And Josh's innocent little voice as he announced, "My daddy gots a gun."

Boone glanced at Eugene and thought he saw the older man stiffen. He might have guessed what was going on, too.

He could have noticed, like Boone had, that Josh didn't call Shelby Mommy. Kidnapping a kid from his legal guardian was serious stuff, if that's what Shelby had done. But if this guy was on the up-and-up, he would have asked the patrolman at the barricades to help him find Shelby and Josh.

Holding his breath, Boone waited for Eugene's answer. Even if Eugene refused to give the guy any information, the way he refused could tip the guy off that Shelby was here.

Eugene adjusted his glasses and paused. "Don't believe I've seen anybody matching that description," he said, smooth as butter.

Boone wanted to leap across the counter and kiss Eugene on both cheeks.

"I know the woman you're talking about," Norma said, coming out of the back room.

Boone's stomach tightened. If only Norma had stayed asleep.

"She came through about noon," Norma continued.

Now Boone had two people he wanted to hug. Not only was Norma covering for Shelby, she was misdirecting this guy.

"Yeah?" The man sat up straighter. "What did she look like?"

"Blond, pretty. The little boy was blond, too. They stopped in to get some food, but they took it to go because they wanted to get over the pass before the snow started."

The guy's fist hit the counter. "Damn it to hell." Then he sighed. "At least I guessed right on which road she'd take."

Norma gazed at him, her expression bland. "She must be important to you."

"Oh, she's important, all right," he replied with a sneer. "She took my kid."

"Goodness!" Norma sounded concerned, but her gaze had no warmth in it. "Have you notified the authorities?"

"Hell, the *authorities* couldn't find their ass with their own two hands. This is one slick chick."

Boone didn't think so. Shelby wasn't enough of a criminal to think of hiding her identity or Josh's. Fear was driving her, not cunning. She was running as fast as she could go and improvising a plan along the way. But he didn't think she was a match for this man.

Boone stood and stretched. Then he faked a yawn. "Well, folks, now that I've had my bedtime snack, I believe I'll go to my room and turn in."

Eugene covered his look of surprise quickly. "Might as well. They won't be opening that road until daybreak, maybe later."

The man looked at Boone. "You've been letting a bed go to waste? Hell, if you don't want it, I'll take it."

"Sorry." Boone clapped his Stetson on his head and pulled on his jacket. "I got here first." He gestured toward the booth where he'd left the pillow and blanket. "But the Sloans put out a blanket and a pillow in case anybody stumbled in during the night. I'm sure you're welcome to that."

The man eyed the setup and turned back to his coffee cup. "We'll see if I get that desperate," he said sourly.

Boone waved at Eugene and Norma and headed out the café door. Once outside he turned up his collar and held onto his hat as he ducked his head and trudged forward against the bitter wind. Snow sifted down inside his jacket and his bare hand grew numb. Once he warned Shelby about the man in the café, he wondered what the heck he was going to do with himself and whether he had enough gas to run the truck's heater all night.

SHELBY LAY in the double bed next to Josh listening to his steady breathing with a touch of envy. All he needed was a darkened room, a soft bed and his blue "blankie" clutched against his cheek.

How she'd love to escape into the world of childhood, if only for a little while, and feel safe again, safe enough to sleep. Her urge to head for Yellowstone had probably come from that same longing. She remembered staying in a little cabin with her mother and father and Patricia, all of the beds in one big room, like settlers on the prairie. They'd never been so cozy before or since.

There was nothing cozy about this room. The heater had a noisy fan, but it didn't block out the whistling of the wind through a crevice between the door and the frame or the rattling of a loose windowpane. After checking the lock at least twenty times, Shelby had dozed off, only to be awakened when she'd heard someone pounding on a door not far away.

Adrenaline had poured through her, but she hadn't wanted to wake Josh by leaping out of bed. By the time she'd eased over to the window, drawn back the curtain and peered out, the motel courtyard had been empty.

Now she worried about who had been pounding on a door in the middle of the night. She'd probably been foolish to take this well-traveled highway north toward Yellowstone. Early in Patricia's marriage to Mason, soon after Josh was born, Shelby had gone over to their house for dinner. She distinctly remembered reminiscing with Patricia about that Yellowstone trip. They'd talked about the fun stops along the way and how much the family vacation had meant to them.

If Mason remembered, he would know exactly what road to take to find her. She was terrible at this cloak-and-dagger stuff, and she really should give up on Yellowstone. Except it wasn't only Josh's excitement that was guiding her there. The thought of seeing the place again with Josh had become the only bright spot in her otherwise frightening world. She loved the way Josh insisted on calling the geysers "geezers." Maybe he'd mixed up the words when she'd mentioned one of the geysers was called Old Faithful.

The windowpane rattled again. Or was that a different sort of noise? She strained to hear over the whirr of the fan and the whistling of the wind. Then the noise came again. A rapid, soft tapping. On her door.

Her stomach lurched in fear and her heartbeat hammered in her ears as she crept quietly out of bed. The tapping grew slightly louder, as if someone wanted to get her attention without alerting anyone else.

Easing back the curtain a tiny slit, she peered out. Then she gasped in surprise as she recognized Boone, his big shoulders hunched against the cold. Had he come to tell her they'd cleared the road?

Her vulnerability made her hesitate before opening the door. Then she shook off any doubts. After all, she'd received nothing but kindness from this man. Now that she'd become one of the hunted, she'd have to learn to trust her instincts if she planned to survive. Her instincts told her Boone wouldn't harm her or Josh.

Crossing to the door, she unlocked and opened it, belatedly remembering that she wore only a cotton nightgown. The cold took her breath away.

"I have to talk to you," Boone said. His face was in shadow. "Can I—"

"Come in, for heaven's sake," she whispered, stepping back. "It's freezing out." Once he was through the door she closed it, but the room temperature seemed to have dropped thirty degrees in that short time.

"Shebby?" Josh mumbled sleepily from the bed.

She hurried over to the bed and leaned down to tuck his

blue blanket against his cheek. "Go back to sleep, sweetheart. It's only Boone."

"'Kay." And just like that, he snuggled back under the covers and dozed off.

Shelby was amazed. Boone and Josh had spent less than twenty minutes together all told, and Boone now had the little boy's complete trust. She straightened and turned. The room was almost totally dark, but she could make out the cowboy standing right where she'd left him by the door.

A thrill of awareness shot through her. Being alone in the dark with this virile man was the most exciting thing that had happened to her in a long while. He'd probably come over to give her a weather report or the latest information on the road, but for a moment she could fantasize that he'd come because he had a burning need to see her again.

"Do you mind talking in the dark?" she murmured as she walked back toward him. "I don't want to wake Josh."

"That's okay."

The closer she came to him, the more she felt the cold that had settled on his clothes, and it made her shiver. But she wasn't afraid. Maybe some of Josh's instinctive trust in Boone had rubbed off on her, because for the first time since she'd left San Antonio, she felt a little less alone.

She wrapped her arms around her body to ward off the chill and came to stand next to him. She had to move close, so she could keep her voice low. The scent of his aftershave teased her. "What is it?" she asked. "Is the road—"

"No, it's not the road," he said quietly. "Look, I don't mean to mess in your business, but there's a man in the café who might be looking for you and the boy."

She gasped and stepped back, her romantic notions shredded by one simple statement. Oh, God, no. Not right here. She'd lulled herself into believing the weather had protected her. Her stomach began to churn. But maybe Boone was wrong. "What...does he look like?"

"Short, stocky but solid, like he works out. He has a military buzz cut."

Nausea rose in her throat. She turned away and took several long, deep breaths until her stomach settled down a little.

"Do you know him?" Boone asked.

"I know him."

"Is he a threat to you?"

She gazed up into his shadowed face and decided to risk telling him the truth. "I suppose. I have his son."

Boone nodded, as if her honesty set well with him. "I figured. Josh told me his daddy has a gun."

Shelby glanced over her shoulder at the sleeping boy, but he didn't seem to have stirred. She lowered her voice. "Mason Fowler is a horrible person. He beat my sister and—"

He drew in a sharp breath. "Did he kill her? Josh said—"

"No," she whispered quickly. "Patricia divorced him two years ago. She...died in a boating accident with...my parents...four months ago." Shelby shuddered with the effort not to cry. She'd been able to stay strong until now, but this big cowboy was such a comforting presence that she was tempted to give in to her grief.

"I'm sorry." His voice was husky, tender.

"Me, too." She swallowed. "Anyway, Patricia didn't leave a will, so unfortunately Mason has more of a claim to Josh than I do. He's started the paperwork to get custody. I don't think the process is going fast enough for him. A couple of days ago, I felt sure he was ready to take Josh for an outing and just...keep him."

"So he wants the boy."

"Not really." She moved closer to Boone. She told herself it was so that he could hear her low-pitched explanation, but she also wished he'd wrap those strong arms around her. It was a dumb idea, and luckily for both of them, he didn't pick up on her body language.

"Mason wasn't the least interested in visitation rights after the divorce," she continued. "For two years he hardly saw Josh. Now he's pretending to be the perfect daddy. I'm convinced he's only after money. My parents did leave a will, and whoever gets Josh also gets the generous maintenance allowance my parents set up for him."

A growl of disapproval rumbled in Boone's chest, and even though Shelby couldn't see his face, she could feel the tension in his body. His righteous fury at hearing such news warmed her more than a blazing fire could have done.

It gave her the courage to ask the question she'd been dreading the answer to. "Does he guess I'm here somewhere?"

"I don't think so. Eugene said he'd never laid eyes on you and Norma said she'd seen you but you went through about lunchtime and were probably way down the road by now."

"Who are Eugene and Norma?"

"Sorry. The Sloans, the people who own the place."

Shelby stared up at him. "They lied for me? Why would they do that?"

"Protecting the privacy of a customer might be part of it, but I think it's also because they didn't take a shine to this Mason character any more than I did. They might have asked themselves why he's coming after you himself, instead of notifying the police. I wondered that, too."

"Because it's more his style. He'd rather intimidate me personally than trust that the law will be on his side. I have no doubt if he decides I'm in the way of his getting that money, he'll want to eliminate me completely. In some ways, I probably played right into his hands, running like this."

"What was your plan?"

She drew strength from the soft murmur of his voice in the darkness, and the woodsy, masculine scent of him eased her panic. "At first I could only think of getting Josh out of town, and I told him we'd go to Yellowstone. Once we were on the road, I realized we couldn't stay there, so I'd decided to continue north to Canada and get a lawyer up there to help me. But now, if Mason's right here..."

As the shivers started again, she wrapped her arms tighter around her body. "I don't know. Maybe he wanted me to do this. Maybe he's been goading me, hoping I'd take off. And the fact is, he *does* intimidate me. But I can't let him get Josh. I just can't."

Boone stood there in silence for a long time. Finally he blew out a breath. "I guess you'd better let me help you."

They were the sweetest words she'd heard in a long while, yet she couldn't imagine what this cowboy could do. "How?"

"Leave your rental car here and come with me to the Rocking D."

"Your...your ranch?"

"Not mine. It belongs to a good buddy of mine, Sebastian Daniels, and his new wife Matty. It's near Canon City, in a pretty little valley. You'll be safe there while you figure out what you want to do next."

"Oh, Boone, that's a wonderful offer." The idea filled her with such longing she could taste it, but she gathered her strength and pride, wrapping them around her like a cloak. "But I can't bring my troubles to roost at your friend's place, especially if he's a newlywed."

"You don't know Sebastian. If he found out I'd left a defenseless woman and a little boy—"

"I'm not defenseless." She refused to come across as a victim.

"You're not?"

"I took a self-defense class. I can take care of myself."

"Well, that's good," he said patiently. "That's real good. But it's kinda tough taking care of yourself when you have a little shaver to worry about."

She knew that. She just hadn't wanted to think about it. "You have a point there," she admitted reluctantly.

"Anyway, if Sebastian knew I'd left you to fend off some wife-beater by yourself, while taking care of the boy and all, he'd have my hide. Sebastian would want me to bring you to the Rocking D, once he understood the situation."

She struggled to keep a grip on the pride she'd been clinging to so fiercely. She needed a champion, needed one desperately. Two champions sounded like heaven, but she couldn't impose like that. "Sounds as if you and your friend are two in a million."

"Not by a long shot." He sounded embarrassed. "We're a couple of ornery cusses, if you must know. Travis, he's the charming one."

"Travis?"

"Travis Evans. You'll meet him, too. In fact, as long as we get out of here at a decent hour in the morning, you'll get to come to his wedding."

The conversation had taken on an unreal quality. "Boone, hold on a minute. You're planning on putting me, with all my problems, smack-dab in the middle of wedding festivities? You can't do that."

"Like I said, my friends would have a fit if I did anything different."

"Some friends you have, Boone." She was beginning to believe she'd stumbled onto the cowboy equivalent of the Knights of the Round Table. Still, taking advantage of such gallantry wasn't her style. "Listen, you're wonderful to offer, but I simply can't put you or your friends to that kind of trouble."

"Okay." His tone was patient. "What's your alternative?"

Good question. She thought of Mason lurking in the café, coiled like a rattlesnake ready to strike. She could watch for him to leave before she ventured out of the room in the morning, but that would mean being trapped without any way of getting food for Josh. Explaining that problem to Josh without telling him about Mason would be tricky.

She faced the fact that she had no plan unless someone offered to be her ally. Boone had offered. "I guess my biggest problem is how to get food to Josh if the road doesn't open right away in the morning," she said.

"I can help you with that."

"I would appreciate it." She was embarrassed by how constrained her position was. She tried for an attitude of independence and self-reliance. "Once Mason leaves, Josh and I can be on our way. Kind as your gesture is, we really wouldn't need to go with you."

He sighed. "Shelby, I've seen the guy. He's a tough customer, and he won't stay fooled forever. Sooner or later, he'll catch on and come back looking for you. When he does, your self-defense courses aren't going to do you much good. If you really want to keep Josh out of his hands, you need help."

She knew he was right. Damn it, he was so right. She'd been foolish to think she could protect Josh by herself. Reckless and foolish. Humbled by her monumental ability to miscalculate, she finally understood that her pride could endanger Josh. Because she loved him far more than her stupid pride, she had no choice but to be indebted to Boone and his friends. "Okay," she said softly. "But I'll find a way to make it up to you. I'll—"

"No need," he said. "Don't even worry about it."

Of course she would. The debt already sat heavy in her chest. But Josh was more important than her own comfort zone right now. "What about my rental car?" she asked.

"You can call the office in Santa Fe and tell them you were afraid to drive it over the pass. That makes sense. You shouldn't drive it over the pass, at least not for a day or two. But you can say you found other transportation. They might charge you something extra if they have to come get it, but—"

"I don't care about that."

"Okay, then it's settled." He turned toward the door. "I'll come over here in the morning when I'm sure Mason's gone."

"Wait a minute." She'd been so caught up in her own problems that she hadn't thought about how Boone had engineered this visit to her room. "Mason's in the café, right?"

"Right."

"When you left, where did he think you were going?"

"To my room."

She gazed at him standing by the door. "But you don't have a room."

"He doesn't know that."

"You can't go back in the café now, can you?"

"No, but I'll be okay in my truck."

His willingness to sacrifice himself for someone he'd just met left her speechless. Finally she recovered enough to stop him before he opened the door. "You will not sleep in the truck, Boone. Share the bed with Josh. He doesn't take up much room. It's the least—"

"Not in this lifetime."

The steel in his words told her it was useless to argue the point. "Okay, then take the chair, or the floor. But you are not going out to that truck. If you do, then the deal's off. I won't go with you to the Rocking D."

"But...you don't know me."

She smiled at that. "Yes, I do. Stay with Josh and me for the rest of the night, Boone. I feel rotten enough about the trouble I'm causing you. Let me at least offer you shelter from this storm."

"You shouldn't feel bad. You're not the one causing the problem. Fowler is."

"Well, I do feel bad, and I wouldn't be able to sleep a wink knowing I sent you out to stay in your truck tonight."

He hesitated. "Well—"

"You'll be doing me a big favor." She pressed her advantage. His only weakness seemed to be his very soft heart. "I haven't been able to sleep hardly at all since I left San Antonio. I have a feeling with you here, I'll be able to finally relax."

"Then go on back to bed." Boone took off his jacket and hat before settling down in the room's only chair. "Don't be afraid to sleep. I'll keep you safe."

4

BOONE SHIFTED his chair so that it blocked the door, just in case. Then he leaned back and closed his eyes, although he didn't expect to sleep. The room was too full of Shelby—her flowery scent, her soft breathing, her rustling movements as she turned over in bed.

His sexual urges were coming out of hibernation, and the timing sucked. For the first time in more than a year, he was seriously interested in a woman. But in spite of the lousy timing, he was somewhat reassured by the ache in his groin. After Darlene had dumped him, he'd felt more like a steer than a bull, except, apparently, when he'd downed a pint of good Irish whiskey and taken Jessica to bed. That hardly counted.

This counted. Nothing about Shelby reminded him of Darlene. Darlene was tall and big-boned, with brown eyes and hair. And damned impatient about getting a ring on her finger. He'd wanted to wait awhile to get married, so he could save enough money to give her a better style of life. At least that's what he'd assumed was his motivation. Sebastian had thought all along he was stalling because deep down he wasn't sure Darlene was the one.

No matter what the reason, his method of operation hadn't suited Darlene, and he'd lost her. Maybe she hadn't been the one, but she'd been a big part of his life for a good many years, and he still couldn't think of her without getting a lump in his throat.

Except now he could. Boone's eyes snapped open as he realized he'd been thinking about Darlene for several minutes, and his throat felt perfectly fine. Testing himself, he conjured up the pictures that usually sent him into deep depression—Darlene in a wedding dress, Darlene standing in front of the preacher with Chester Littlefield, Darlene and Chester in bed together.

The scenes that had once evoked such morbid curiosity and deep pain barely kept his attention now. Instead his thoughts were firmly anchored on Shelby. When he'd first seen her, he'd been fascinated with the way her hair spilled out of her perky ponytail, so silky and blond, reminding him of a corn tassel. The bounce of her hair when she moved had made him smile.

But tonight when she'd opened her door to him, he'd had no urge to smile. Instead his mouth had gone dry and his heart had begun to pound. In the light from the motel courtyard she'd looked like an angel, pure and untouched in her simple cotton nightgown with her hair falling gently to her shoulders.

Then his attention had settled on the swell of her breasts under the soft flannel, and he'd forgotten about angels and started thinking of naked bodies writhing on hot sheets. The urge to protect her had brought him to her door, but once there, he'd fought the equally powerful urge to claim her as his, to put her in an ivory tower away from the reach of other men. But within *his* easy reach.

Boone didn't generally believe in impulse, and he hadn't acted on it this time, either. Instead of pulling her into his arms and branding her with his kisses, a concept that made him tremble with temptation, he'd stood just inside the door while she went over to quiet the boy.

By the time she'd come back to stand in front of him, he'd had better control of himself. Marginally better. He'd still wanted to skim off her nightgown and make love to her until his name poured from her lips in a moan of delight. Totally uncharacteristic of him. His buddies would never believe he'd had such wild thoughts about a woman he'd just met.

But he did. She'd never know how hard he'd clenched his hands at his sides to keep from reaching for her, especially when she'd told him about her sister and her folks. She might have appreciated the comfort of a man's strong arms at that moment, but he hadn't trusted himself to keep his touch confined to comfort.

He'd have to be mighty careful in the next few days while he helped her sort out her problem. And no matter how much he might want to be, he couldn't be her solution. His first obligation was to Elizabeth and Jessica.

Shelby's breathing took on a slow, steady rhythm, and Boone dared to open his eyes and glance over to where she and Josh slept. The glowing red numbers on the bedside clock showed him it was after three in the morning. He really should try to sleep, too, but he couldn't stop looking at Shelby.

A sliver of light from a break in the curtains angled across the bed and shone on her golden hair. It touched the line of her jaw and moved across to pick out a narrow section of Josh's tousled curls.

The boy would help keep him straight, Boone thought. Without Josh in that bed, the impulse to climb in with her would be too great. But Josh was there.

Then, abruptly, both the red numbers on the clock and the light from the window winked out, and the heater fan whirled to a stop.

Boone muttered a curse. The storm had knocked out the power.

"Come back on, damn it," he muttered under his breath,

but the world had fallen silent except for Shelby and Josh's quiet breathing. Boone figured these motel units were made of cardboard and chewing gum. He could already feel the chill seeping through the wall behind him, and soon the room would be very cold.

Putting on his jacket and shoving his hands in the pockets, he sat in the chair and waited. Still no heat. Eventually Shelby and Josh began moving restlessly in the bed and Boone knew the cold had penetrated the blankets.

He stood, walked over to the closet and took their coats off the hangers. He arranged the coats over them as best he could. Working carefully so Josh wouldn't wake up, Boone draped Josh's special blanket around the little boy's shoulders. Then he returned to the chair and hunched down into the sheepskin lining of his coat.

The temperature of the room fell a few more degrees and the restless movements from the bed continued. Finally Boone stood again, took off his jacket, and walked toward the bed. Josh had curled up as close to Shelby as he could get. They were both shivering. Boone was, too, but it wasn't as if he hadn't ever been cold in his life. He could stand a little shivering.

The toe of his boot caught the edge of the nightstand, making a clunking noise that must have awakened Shelby, because she turned over and mumbled his name sleepily.

He paused. "I'm here."

"Why is it so cold?"

"Power's out." He leaned down and draped his jacket over her and Josh. "It'll be morning soon. Try and get some rest."

She rose up on one elbow. "What are you doing, covering us with your jacket? You need it," she whispered urgently.

"I'm not cold," he lied.

"But I'm c-cold," Josh said, his teeth chattering. "S-so's B-bob."

Shelby gripped Boone's arm. "Take off your boots and get in here with us."

Panic gripped him. He wasn't sure he could trust himself. "I don't think that's a good—"

"Are you going to stand on ceremony when a little boy is shivering like this?"

"No." He had to risk it, for the boy's sake. "No, I'm not."

"Good." She released her hold on his arm. "Come on, Josh, move over closer to me. Boone's getting in on your side. The heat went out so we have to snuggle to stay warm."

Heart racing, Boone walked around the bed and sat on the edge so he could pull off his boots. The boy would be between them, he reminded himself. But this still felt way too risky.

"I *like* t-to snuggle," Josh said.

"I know you do," Shelby replied, her voice playful as she rustled under the sheets, obviously gathering Josh close to keep him warm. "You're my little snuggle-bunny."

In spite of his misgivings about getting in bed with Josh and Shelby, Boone had always yearned for a scenario exactly like this one. He'd counted on being a husband and a father by now. Darlene had taken away his plan to be a husband, and although he might be Elizabeth's father, nothing about that situation felt good to him. He took off his belt so the cold buckle wouldn't press against Josh.

"I love you, Shebby," Josh said, his voice muffled. "More'n all my Legos."

"I love you, too, sweetheart," she murmured. "More than all my Billy Joel albums."

"I love you more'n all my Tonka trucks."

"I love you more than my salt-and-pepper-shaker collection."

"Even the duck ones?"

"Even the duck ones," Shelby said.

"'Cause I quack you up, huh, Shebby?"

Boone chuckled.

"Exactly," Shelby said. "You totally quack me up."

From the way Josh giggled, Boone knew this must be a game they'd played many times over. He envied their closeness. Shelby and Josh had a good thing going. Mason Fowler had no business coming between them, no matter what his biological rights might be.

"Okay, I'm getting under the covers now," Boone said as he eased into bed next to Josh. The bed was a standard double, too short for him. With Shelby and Josh already in the bed, it was a tight fit.

Balancing on the edge of the mattress, he tried to find a place to put his sock-covered feet and brushed them against Shelby's bare calf. "Oops, sorry." He felt as if he'd touched an electric fence as the jolt of awareness traveled through him. He wondered if she wore anything at all under that nightgown. Probably not. He swallowed.

"Put your feet back over here," Shelby said. "Let me help you warm them up."

"That's okay. They'll warm up on their own." No way was he playing footsie with her under the covers. He laid his head on the pillow and figured if there was more light he'd be looking directly into Shelby's eyes. But as it was, he couldn't see much of anything.

Not being able to see sharpened his other senses, though. He breathed in her perfume mingled with the soapsuds scent of a little boy who'd had a bath only hours before. He tuned in to her breathing, and the rustle of sheets that telegraphed her every move. He scooted closer to Josh.

"You're a ice cube!" Josh shrank away from him.

"Help warm him up," Shelby said. "And then he'll keep you warm."

"Maybe this isn't such a good idea." Boone held himself away from Josh so his chilled clothes wouldn't get the little guy cold. He was about ready to fall on the floor.

"His shirt's cold, Shebby," Josh complained.

"Unsnap your shirt, Boone," Shelby said.

"What?"

"No, really. I read about this. Your skin is a lot warmer than your shirt. Actually the most efficient way for us to maximize body heat would be for everyone to cuddle without any clothes on at all."

Boone choked. "We're not doing that," he said in a raspy voice. He unsnapped his shirt though, because he knew she was right about the most efficient way to transfer body heat.

"No, of course we're not doing that," she said. "I'm just making a point."

"I wanna," Josh said brightly. He started wriggling on the bed.

"No, Josh." Shelby held him still. "Keep your pajamas on."

"Why?"

"Because it's not necessary to take them off. We'll be fine."

"But I would *like* it."

"I'm sure you would, you little streaker." She chuckled. "Josh grabs any opportunity at all to take his clothes off, don't you, buddy?"

"Yep."

All this talk about nakedness naturally led Boone to think of undressing Shelby, which wasn't helpful. But he smiled at the picture of Josh running bare-assed through the house. He'd forgotten how little kids loved to do that, and how much joy they took in the simplest of things. Their world could be uncomplicated and filled with wonder, so long as some adult didn't mess it up for them.

Without warning, Josh laid his small hand on Boone's chest. "Now you're warm," he said.

The trusting acceptance of that casual touch was deeply moving. "Good," Boone said.

"Let's cuddle," Josh said.

"We are cuddling," Boone said.

"Uh-uh. You gots to be closer."

Boone edged farther onto the mattress.

"You gots to put your arm around us," Josh said. "'Cause you're the biggest."

Boone wasn't too sure about the wisdom of wrapping his arm around Shelby and Josh. And Shelby had suddenly become very quiet over there. Maybe she was rethinking this, herself. He hesitated.

"Come *on*," Josh said, grabbing his arm. "Don'tcha know how to cuddle?"

He did know. In fact, he was hungry for the chance. With a sigh of resignation, he reached over Josh and slipped an arm around Shelby. As he drew them both into the shelter of his embrace, Shelby's breath caught.

So this bothers her some, too. Boone's ego welcomed the boost. Given a choice, he wouldn't have put either of them in this position, but with the power out, he had no choice. He closed his eyes and savored the pleasure of holding Shelby, even if they did have a three-year-old between them.

"Now you, Shebby," Josh said.

"Okay." Her voice sounded husky.

Boone nearly stopped breathing when she hesitantly brushed her hand across his rib cage. With the way he'd pulled his shirt open, she had no option but to slide her hand underneath it as she wrapped her arm partway around him.

He couldn't believe that such a small hand could have such a huge impact on his system. Sparks of excitement sent off a chain reaction throughout his body.

While Boone was still dealing with the sweet pressure of Shelby's handprint on his skin, Josh pressed his ear against Boone's chest, right over his heart. "It's beating," he said.

"I should hope so," Boone answered.

"Fast. Thumpity, thumpity, thumpity."

"I guess that's what the cold does to you," Boone said.

Then Josh turned and pressed his other ear against Shelby's chest. "You must be cold, too, Shebby."

"Mmm." Her hand stayed very, very still.

Light though her touch was, he felt the imprint of each of her fingers. He even imagined the spiral patterns of her fingerprints leaving a mark on his skin.

"I like this." Josh sounded sleepy.

"Good," Shelby said. "Now go to sleep."

"'Kay."

Boone loved the sound of Shelby's voice in the dark. He loved the warmth of her body inside the circle of his arm while the wind howled and battered at the windows and the snow covered the world in white. He loved the delicate pressure of her fingers against his back. Sure, sex was on his mind, but his body wasn't raging out of control. Mostly he felt incredibly right being here in this tiny bed with her and Josh, keeping them safe.

He'd known them for such a short time, and yet he felt as if he'd slipped into the most perfect spot in the universe. He hadn't thought he could sleep in such a cramped bed with such a tempting woman so close, but gradually contentment crept through him, lulling him into one of the deepest sleeps of his life.

"VROOOM! Vrrrrooom-vrooooom! Beep, beep!"

Shelby woke to the familiar sound of Josh playing toy cars on the floor beside her bed and the unfamiliar sensation of being cuddled spoon-fashion against a very big, very aroused male body. From the steady sound of Boone's breathing, she was sure he was still asleep.

But his sexual instincts were wide awake. His erection pressed against her bottom, and his arm shifted slightly so that his big hand cupped her breast. The contact felt... wonderful.

Daylight seeped in around the closed curtains and the bedside clock blinked rapidly, flashing twelve o'clock. The heater fan whirred and clanked, so it was no real surprise that the room was warm once again. Power had been restored.

But Shelby was more interested in a different sort of power, the sexual kind issuing from the man cradling her body in his. Boone would be very embarrassed if he knew what he was doing, she thought with a soft smile. Apparently both of them had been so exhausted they hadn't awakened when Josh climbed out of bed. They'd simply shifted positions.

Shelby liked this position. In a minute she'd need to slide out from under Boone's arm and get out of bed before he realized how forward he'd been with her. But for now, she'd close her eyes, draw the sheet up to her chin and pretend to sleep a little while longer so that she could enjoy her fantasy.

She'd never quite admitted to herself that she had a fantasy man in mind, but during that childhood trip to Yellowstone she'd wandered away from the cabin and become lost. A cowboy on horseback had found her and returned her, scared and crying, to her family. He might not have been a very large man, but to a kid of seven, he had seemed enormous in his boots and ten-gallon hat.

Maybe that cowboy was one of the reasons she hadn't ever fallen in love enough to consider marrying. Maybe all along she'd been hoping to find her big, brave cowboy again. What a silly, girlish dream. And yet, lying here tucked against Boone, she didn't feel the least bit silly or girlish. In fact, if Josh weren't in the room, she'd stay right in this bed and see what happened when the big guy woke up.

He might be shy at first, and that fit right in with her fantasy because it meant that he didn't have tons of experience with women. She suspected that when this man gave his heart, he gave it for keeps. He would be a tender and considerate lover, but if a woman knew how to push the right buttons, she'd bet that he'd turn into a real force of nature.

A picture of Boone filled with wild passion certainly got her juices flowing. Considering the size of the erection pressing against her, he might even be a little scary. Her heart beat faster with a mixture of excitement and trepidation. Ah, but he was also a gentle man. The combination of size, power and gentleness was nearly irresistible to her.

Beneath the hand he'd cupped over her breast, her nipple tightened. Okay, she needed to get out of this bed *now*, before she embarrassed herself, as well as Boone. Shifting her weight slightly, she took hold of his wrist and tried to move his arm away. It was like trying to lift a felled tree.

His arm didn't budge, but his fingers flexed against her breast.

She closed her eyes again, trembling slightly. His touch felt so good. She'd been so focused on Josh since—well, really since he'd been born—that she'd had no social life, let alone a man in her bed. The guy she'd been seeing when Josh was born hadn't been interested in babies and couldn't understand why she'd felt such a responsibility for her nephew. After she'd broken off that relationship, she hadn't bothered to cultivate another.

Under different circumstances, she wouldn't mind culti-vating this one. But she couldn't get involved with Boone, not when she needed all her energy to keep Josh safe. With regret, she got a stronger grip on Boone's wrist and at-tempted to pull his arm away.

Still no dice. He moaned her name softly and pulled her in tighter, pressing the crotch of his jeans hard against her bottom. Her pulse raced as she wondered if he was only fak-ing sleep. But no, his soft snoring told her he was truly zonked. At least the name he'd mumbled was hers. That gave her a great deal of satisfaction.

But he was too strong for her to budge him. She hadn't fully realized just how strong he was, and without his brain and conscience in gear, his basic needs had taken over, keeping her prisoner. She'd have to wake him up.

She shook his arm as best she could, considering it was wrapped around her like a steel band. "Boone. Wake up."

Josh scrambled to his feet and came to the edge of the bed to stare at her. "I woked up."

"I see that." She was glad the covers disguised the grip Boone had on her breast, although Josh wouldn't think any-thing of it. After all, a three-year-old didn't know anything about sex between a man and a woman.

"I goed potty and then I played trucks."

"Good for you. You're a big boy. Boone! Isn't Josh a big boy?"

"Huh?" Boone came awake with a start, released her breast as if it had burned his hand, and fell out of the far side of the bed with a terrific thud.

5

BOONE HAD his boots on, his shirt snapped and his coat buttoned faster than his buddy Travis could rope and tie a calf, and Travis was known for his speed. "I'll check on breakfast," he said as he clapped his hat on his head and charged out the motel room door.

He hadn't dared look at Shelby, and one quick glance at Josh confirmed that the little boy was staring at him as if he'd just grown ears and a tail. Which he practically had.

Damn! How had he ended up plastered against Shelby's backside, clutching a handful of her breast? What had happened to the kid who was supposed to sleep between them and keep everything respectable and proper? Who told that boy he could get out of bed, anyway?

And that was another thing. Boone, the macho protector who had assigned himself the job of staying alert to the slightest danger threatening either the boy or the woman, hadn't even realized when Josh had left the bed. Boone had promised to keep watch. Some guardian he'd turned out to be.

He snorted in disgust at himself as he stomped through knee-high drifts toward the café. The sun was out and the sound of heavy machinery from down the road indicated the snowplows were working. Most of the cars and trucks that had been parked at the motel the night before were gone. Squinting up at the sun, Boone judged the time to be around nine in the morning. Late. Fowler should already be on his way to Colorado Springs.

Boone's face still felt hot with embarrassment, so he paused, leaned down and scooped up a handful of snow to pat over his cheeks. He used to think he couldn't trust himself when he drank. Now apparently he couldn't trust himself when he slept, either.

He'd been having a dynamite dream about Shelby, which must have been inspired by the way he was groping her in his sleep. He wondered how long he'd been doing it, how long she'd had to endure his fumblings while she tried to escape without making a big deal of it in front of Josh.

In those first groggy seconds of waking up, he'd been aware of two things—a full erection shoved right up against Shelby's soft bottom, and the weight of her breast cradled in his left hand. The pleasure of both sensations had lasted for the space of a breath. Then his brain had cleared enough to allow humiliation to come roaring through to destroy that pleasure completely.

An apology was definitely in order, but he couldn't picture himself trying that maneuver in front of Josh. No telling what Josh would think he was trying to apologize for. In Josh's world there was nothing wrong with people "snuggling" together.

Boone wondered what Shelby must be thinking right now and groaned aloud. Maybe she'd refuse to go with him to the Rocking D, figuring she'd take her chances on her own rather than trust her safety to a sex maniac.

Well, he couldn't force her to go with him, but he could make sure Fowler was gone before she set out, then follow her until she'd made it over the pass and onto dry pavement. But hell, he wanted her to go with him so he could guarantee she wouldn't run into Fowler. Somehow he had to convince her that he would never, ever lay a hand on her again.

He stomped the snow from his boots before walking into the café. A gray-haired woman he'd never seen before was behind the counter serving coffee to a couple of men in heavy coats seated on stools. The waitress was probably Edna, Boone decided, remembering the other employee Eugene had talked about. He saw no sign of either of the Sloans, and best of all, no sign of Fowler.

Sitting at the counter next to one of the men, he grabbed a menu from the aluminum holder in front of him. "Guess the road's open, huh?" he commented to the guy beside him.

"Sure is," the man said. "We came through about twenty minutes ago, and they got it cleared pretty good both north and southbound. I hear a few folks were stranded here last night."

"Yep." Boone studied the menu and tried to think what Josh and Shelby might like him to bring them for breakfast. He'd been so hell-bent on getting out of the room he hadn't stopped to ask. He rubbed his chin and reminded himself he needed to get his shaving kit out of the truck.

"Including you?"

"Yep. Say, what do you think a three-year-old boy eats for breakfast?"

The man chuckled. "That's anybody's guess. Mine used to like cold spaghetti."

"Or cold pizza," added the man next to him. "With the cheese congealed into this globby mess on top. My kid loved that for breakfast."

The waitress turned from the coffeemaker. Sure enough, her name was Edna. "Peanut-butter toast is your best bet," she said. "Unless he's allergic to peanuts."

Boone shook his head, dazed at the odds of lousing up such a simple thing as breakfast. "I'll try an order of peanut-butter toast for him," he said. "But I'll find out about the allergy thing before he eats it."

"Okay." Edna took her order pad from her apron and started writing. "This will be to go?"

"Yes. All of it. I'll need two large coffees, the toast, and..." Boone paused to scan the menu again. "Milk," he decided, figuring Josh could drink it and Shelby could use it for her coffee if she took her coffee with cream. He couldn't believe he'd fondled a woman's breast, yet he had no idea how she took her coffee, or even if she drank the stuff.

But her nipple had been tight. Tight and aroused. The tidbit of information must have been buried under layers of his own embarrassment, but when it surfaced, it was a revelation to him. Maybe she hadn't endured his touch, after all. Maybe she'd even liked it. Maybe she'd even *wanted* it.

Well.

"Anything besides the toast, coffee, and milk?" Edna asked.

"Huh?" Boone glanced up in confusion.

"On your order," Edna said, smiling a little. "Or should I get you some coffee first so you can function? I know how I am before my first cup in the morning."

"Uh, no!" He was afraid he was blushing. "I mean, I can finish up the order without a cup of coffee. Let's see—how about two orders of scrambled eggs, hash browns, bacon, and a couple of sweet rolls?"

Edna's smile broadened. "Working up an appetite, are you? Want any juice?"

"Yeah, juice. Orange. Three glasses. That should do it." He closed the menu with a decisive snap. As it turned out, he did have an appetite, now that the idea of returning to the room and facing Shelby wasn't quite so embarrassing. Maybe she'd been turned on, too. She might even have been the one who'd cuddled up to him, once Josh had climbed out of bed.

Both of them had been under a strain. If they'd needed a little human contact, they couldn't be blamed for that. He certainly didn't blame Shelby.

The two men paid for their coffee and left, wishing him a good trip. While his breakfast order was cooking, Boone paid a quick visit to the café's rest room. He looked like a goddamned derelict, he thought, grimacing at his reflection and trying to finger-comb his hair.

And he continued to think about Shelby's nipple. If her nipple had been like that, then maybe the rest of her had responded, too. She might have been lying there all warm and damp and ready.

He might never know, but he sure felt good thinking that she might have. And if things were different, if he didn't have Elizabeth and Jessica to consider, then he'd have devoted some effort to finding out how she reacted if he touched her like that again. As it was, he'd better not try it. He was in no position to start something he couldn't finish.

His order was packaged and ready when he returned to the counter. As he headed out the door of the café with two paper sacks, Eugene walked in. He looked tired, but he'd obviously taken the time to shave, shower and change clothes. Boone felt grungy in comparison. Once he'd taken care of breakfast, he really had to see about cleaning up. He wondered if he dared risk using the shower in Shelby's room, or if that was asking for more trouble.

"Hey, Boone," Eugene said. "Glad to see you made it through the night okay."

"Yeah, I, uh, did."

Eugene lowered his voice. "You went to warn that young woman when you left here last night, didn't you?"

"Yeah. That guy creeped me out."

"Me, too, but then I couldn't figure out where you were going to sleep. Did you spend the night in your truck?"

Boone shifted his weight from one foot to the other. "Actually, she—well, she needed someone to sort of guard her and the boy, so I stayed."

Eugene smiled. "Good." He glanced at the sacks Boone was holding. "Breakfast for all of you?"

"Yeah."

"Well, I won't keep you, then. But if it makes you feel any better, that fellow was one of the first ones out of here. He took off the minute the snowplow came through."

Boone nodded. "Did you happen to notice what he was driving?"

"Sure did. Black Land Rover. Fancy."

"That's good to know. Thanks. Listen, I'll be taking Shelby and Josh with me and she's going to leave her rental car here." He hoped Shelby hadn't reconsidered the plan because of what happened between them in bed. But he had to go on the assumption that she still wanted his help. "We'll call somebody to come up from Santa Fe to get the car, but I wanted you to know."

Eugene's smile deepened. "Sounds like you're doing a little rescue work yourself. Like that lighthouse thing you talked about last night. Or in your case, maybe it's more like a knight in shining armor."

"I'm going to try." After last night, Boone figured his armor was tarnished, but he still intended to keep Shelby and Josh safe.

Eugene gripped Boone's upper arm and gave it a squeeze. "You're a good man, Boone. Stop by any time you're on this road. I'll buy you a cup of coffee."

"Thanks." Boone returned Eugene's smile. "I'll look forward to that."

THE MINUTE Boone was out the door Shelby had got dressed in record time and then helped Josh into his clothes. After they were totally ready and nearly all packed, she'd neatly made the bed, thinking that would help Boone feel less awkward when he returned. She smoothed the spread so that it looked as if no one had slept there, let alone cuddled and fondled and enjoyed...oh, she had to stop thinking about that.

But no matter how hard she tried, she couldn't seem to put the thought of Boone's hand on her breast or the bulge of his erection out of her mind. When he knocked on the door, she was *still* thinking about it. She glanced out the window to make sure it was him, and the sight of his big, beautiful body made her palms sweat.

Josh had scrambled up to the chair to look out the window with her. "Boone's here!" he shouted and ran to the door to fumble with the lock. "He gots presents!"

"Food," Shelby said, going over to help him with the lock. Josh's eagerness broke her heart. She wondered how she'd ever console the little boy when he had to tell his new friend goodbye. "It's only breakfast, Josh."

Josh threw open the door. "Hi, Boone! Whatcha gots for me and you?"

Boone grinned at Josh as he walked through the door with the bags balanced in one arm and his free hand behind his back. "Wait'll you see," he said as Shelby closed the door behind him.

Josh started jumping up and down. "What, Boone? What, what, what?"

He crouched down in front of Josh and brought his hand forward. "A snowball."

Josh gasped in wonder and reached out a finger to poke at the glistening white ball. "Brrrr!" He glanced at Boone. "Can we throw it?"

"Sure. If Shelby will open the door again for a minute, you can throw it right outside."

Shelby followed instructions and opened the door. Now that the sun had come out, it wasn't nearly as cold, anyway.

"Go ahead, Josh," Boone coaxed. "Pick it up."

Josh made one attempt to hold the snowball and dropped it back in Boone's hand with a squeal.

"Just do it fast," Boone said.

"Awright." Josh grabbed up the snowball and pitched it about three feet beyond the doorway. "I did it! I throwed a snowball, Shebby!" He danced up and down and waved his cold hand. "I throwed it out there. Right there. Can you see it?"

"I sure can."

"Bob wants to throw one."

"Oh, I forgot." Boone reached in the pocket of his coat and took out an imaginary object. Here's Bob's snowball."

Josh peered down at Boone's palm. "Yup. There it is. Throw it, Bob."

"I'd better close the door now," Shelby said. "We're letting out the heat."

"Wait!" Josh said. "Bob gots to throw his."

"Okay. But tell Bob to hurry."

Josh studied the open doorway. "Okay. He throwed it."

"Then let's close the door." As she pushed it shut she dared to glance down at Boone still crouched on the floor. She discovered him gazing up at her. He was practically kneeling at her feet.

Silently he mouthed the words *I'm sorry.*

Her heart did a somersault. God, his eyes were green. "It's okay," she murmured softly. Then she took a deep breath and spoke normally. "Well, I guess we need to eat, huh?"

"Yeah, before it gets cold." He broke eye contact and levered himself to his feet. "I hope you don't mind about the snowball, but I thought maybe, if Josh had never played in the snow, he'd—"

"I wanna play in the snow!" Josh tugged on her hand and looked up at her with pleading blue eyes. "*Please*, Shebby? Can me and Bob *please* play in the snow?"

Boone stepped closer to her and lowered his voice. "It's all clear."

Shelby looked quickly at Boone and was once again drawn in by the beauty of his eyes. They reminded her of a summer meadow, lush and tempting. "You're sure?"

Boone nodded.

Shelby couldn't look away. Boone's gaze was so warm, so full of life. Slowly Josh's pleading voice faded from her awareness as her attention drifted to Boone's mouth. She imagined at first it would settle tenderly over hers, but as he caught fire, his kiss would become more demanding. Then he'd move from kissing her lips to kissing other parts of her body, and...

"*Shebby.*" Josh hung his whole weight from her hand, nearly pulling her over.

Dazed, she looked down at the little boy. "What is it, Josh?"

Josh spoke with great deliberation. "Can...me...and... Bob...play...in...the...snow?"

"Maybe for a little while. After we eat some breakfast."

"Whoopee!" He started running around the room. "Snow, snow, snow, snow."

"Okay, settle down." She caught him by the shoulder as he ran past.

"Might be a good idea at that," Boone said. "To play awhile after breakfast. He can work off some of that excess energy before he gets into the truck."

Josh stopped his wiggling and stared up at Boone. "What truck?"

"You and Shelby are going to ride with me to the Rocking D."

"The *ranch*?" Josh's eyes widened. "Where you gots *horsies*?"

"That's right."

Josh turned slowly and looked up at Shelby. "We really are?" he whispered, as if he couldn't believe such good fortune.

Her heart wrenched. Perhaps this was a terrible idea. The more time Josh spent with Boone, the harder their eventual separation would be. She should probably tell Boone that she'd changed her mind. They'd drive the little rental car on through Colorado and into Wyoming, as she'd intended.

"Shelby."

The sound of her name spoken in Boone's deep, gentle voice sent shivers of pleasure up her spine. She glanced at him.

He cleared his throat. "I know what you're probably thinking. Listen, please don't let what happened last night.... Well, it won't ever happen again." He swallowed. "I swear to God it won't. You need to come to the Rocking D. Everything will work out better that way."

She wished they were alone so she could let him know that what had happened last night, or rather early this morning, hadn't bothered her a bit. Poor guy, he thought she was offended and that's why she was hesitating. She could hardly explain in front of Josh, especially considering that her main concern was for the little boy. She didn't want him to get his heart broken.

But neither could she send away a good man like Boone, letting him think he'd horrified her with his perfectly natural urges. They needed time to sort out this tangle, and a day or so at the Rocking D might be the answer for that.

Besides, given a little time, maybe she could figure out a way to keep some contact with Boone, for Josh's sake. Once she and Josh knew where the ranch was, they might be able to go back for a visit someday, after the mess with Mason Fowler had been handled. The thought cheered her. She'd like to reconnect with Boone once she was no longer on the run. Something might even come of it.

She looked down at Josh, who stood there with a very worried expression on his face. "We'll go to the Rocking D for a day or so," she said. "Long enough for you to ride a horse, Josh."

Josh beamed as he looked from Shelby to Boone and back to Shelby again. "Me and Bob, we're gonna *love* it there," he said.

As she absorbed the happiness shining from the little boy's eyes, Shelby found tears gathering in hers. He so needed a wonderful man in his life, a man like Boone. Come to think of it, she wouldn't mind having a wonderful man like Boone in her life, either.

"Well, now," she said, forcing cheer into her voice as she quickly blinked away the tears. "We'd better get going. We have lots to do before we get on the road!"

6

SHELBY INSISTED Boone use her calling card to phone his friends at the Rocking D and explain the situation. Then she looked for an excuse to vacate the room while he shaved and showered, and came up with an errand she and Josh could run. They'd head for the café to get plastic bags to tape over their shoes so they could play in the snow more easily. She even mentioned she might stay for a cup of coffee or hot chocolate.

But even hot chocolate couldn't sway Josh. The little boy begged to stay with Boone, which showed how much he was beginning to attach himself to the big cowboy. Shelby could see the way Josh constantly watched Boone, looking for clues as to how a man behaved. Shelby finally gave in and left him there. After all, she was the only one who needed to get far away from the erotic pull of having a sexy man in her shower.

Norma Sloan was behind the counter when Shelby walked in, and she hauled out the café's lost-and-found box. The box produced mittens and boots that would work for Josh, and an old pair of boots, a stocking cap and some gloves for Shelby.

Caught up in the excitement of such unexpected treasures, Shelby forgot to stay for coffee. She remembered after she was out the door but decided not to worry about it. Boone probably took quick showers.

On the way back to the room, she noticed his truck for the

first time. She identified it easily because his name was on it, painted on the side panel of the door. Boone Connor, Farrier. So he was a blacksmith. That fit him, she decided. The job seemed to be made for someone who was both strong and gentle.

She continued on to the room, eager to share her success, and opened the motel door without thinking to knock. "Hey, guys, you'll never believe what I—" She came to a screeching halt and almost dropped the boots at the breathtaking sight that greeted her through the open bathroom door. Boone, naked except for a towel knotted around his hips, was helping Josh pretend to shave. Tension curled deliciously within her.

Boone turned immediately, and a dull red crept over his cheeks. He'd probably meant to be dressed by now, but Josh had slowed him down. "Uh, don't worry," he mumbled. "I took the blade out."

"Oh. Okay." She hadn't gotten far enough in her thinking to be worried about that. She was too busy assimilating the picture Boone made. And salivating. She might have known his chest hair would be dark, curly and thick. And talk about a hard body. The blacksmithing job kept him very fit indeed. She grew warm just looking at all that muscle. Much more of this view and she'd be ready to attack him.

The bathroom mirror was still fogged, but he'd rubbed a clean spot so that Josh could see himself from where he was kneeling on the vanity, a towel tied around his neck to protect his clothes. While Boone steadied him with an arm around his waist, he carefully stroked the shaving cream from his face with Boone's razor.

"I'm shavin', Shebby!" Josh called out. "See me?"

"I see you." But she had a tough time concentrating on her nephew.

She should turn away, but she didn't have the willpower.

Not only was he beautiful in body, but his sensitive treat-
ment of Josh displayed a beautiful spirit, too. Pride radiated
from Josh as he carefully worked the razor in obvious imitation of the way he'd watched Boone do it. He'd probably
pestered Boone the whole time the big guy was in the
shower, until Boone had finally given up and agreed to help
him shave when he got out.

She imagined Boone in the shower. With no towel.... She
almost groaned aloud. If Josh hadn't been here... But he
was. He most certainly was.

Shelby wondered if Boone realized that Josh would now
be his slave for life. In all his three years, Josh had never had
a man take as much time for him as Boone had in the past
few hours. Shelby had given him all the attention she could,
but some things were beyond her. Teaching him how to
shave was only one in a long list of male-oriented activities.

No doubt about it, she'd need to find a way to keep Boone
a part of Josh's life. The two had taken to each other from the
beginning.

Boone cleared his throat. "What did you find?" he asked,
keeping his attention on Josh.

Bless his heart, he was trying to keep this moment from
being awkward, for Josh's sake.

"Uh, boots." She held them up, even though he wasn't
looking in her direction. Damn, but he was gorgeous. He'd
already surpassed her fantasies about big strong cowboys,
and now he looked like the perfect father, too. "Mrs. Sloan
had a lost-and-found box under the counter and these were
in there. She also had mittens for Josh and some gloves for
me."

"Good." Boone gazed into the mirror. "How're you coming, there, buddy?"

"Almost done." Josh had shaving cream everywhere—all
over the towel and dabbed on the mirror and the sink, even

on Boone's chest, but he'd managed to get most of it off his face.

"Looks good," Boone said. He reached over and snagged a hand towel from the rack. He rubbed it over his chest before handing it to Josh. "Wipe with this. Then you can slap on some shaving lotion."

"Yeah." Josh nodded. "Shavin' lotion." He wiped his face and peered at himself in the mirror. "All shaved."

"Okay. Down we go." Boone lifted Josh effortlessly from the sink using only the arm he had wrapped around the little boy's waist. He acted as if Josh were no heavier than a feather.

Shelby knew better. She'd hefted Josh enough times to know how much he weighed. She watched in fascination as Boone's back muscles flexed with the motion. She'd give her entire salt-and-pepper-shaker collection to feel those muscles move under her hand.

Boone untied the towel from around Josh's neck, careful to keep his gaze on the boy and not let it stray toward Shelby. "Now hold out your hands, like this." Boone cupped his hands in front of him.

Josh mirrored him perfectly. Shelby thought what a wonderful video this would have made. She'd left her camera back in her apartment because it hadn't seemed necessary under the circumstances. Now she was sorry, although Boone would never have agreed to be filmed, now that she thought about it.

"I'm going to sprinkle some shaving lotion in your hands," Boone said, "but don't do anything yet. We'll slap it on together."

"*Okay.*" Josh gazed up at his idol with reverence.

Boone shook some lotion into his own hand. "First you rub your hands together like this," he said, demonstrating. "Then slap your cheeks like this." He patted his face briskly.

Josh clapped his hands against his cheeks and grinned. Then he ran over to Shelby. "Smell!"

She crouched down, put her nose against Josh's cheek and took a deep sniff. "Mmm, good," she said. "Good enough to eat." She nibbled his ear.

"Don't bite on me!" Josh said, giggling.

"I can't help it," Shelby said. "You smell so good." Now if only Boone would let her do the same thing, her world would be complete.

Instead he closed the bathroom door. "I'll be out in a minute," he called. "You two can start putting on your boots."

Shelby glanced at the closed door and sighed. The show was over.

MASON FOWLER calculated that he had some heavy-duty driving to do before he could hope to catch up with that bitch Shelby. She'd probably stopped for the night somewhere around Colorado Springs, but by now she'd be back on the road, hell-bent for Wyoming. Good thing her apartment manager had told him about Yellowstone. If he had anything to do with it, she'd never make it that far.

She was a sentimental little twit, and not all that smart about covering her tracks. As if a rental car would throw him off. All he had to do was look for a Texas plate on a compact sedan and see if she and Josh were in it. He figured she was about two or three hours ahead of him, but he'd make that up. She wasn't the type to speed and he made good use of his fuzz-buster.

Once he found her, he'd force her off the road and take the kid. Any court in the country would back him on that one. Aunt kidnaps man's only son, man goes berserk and chases woman until he gets his kid back. Aunt loses custody. She'd played right into his hands, exactly as he'd hoped she would if he crowded her long enough.

The only thing he hadn't counted on was the snowstorm. But the folks at the café had been real helpful. At least he knew for sure she was on this road, which had to mean she was going for the Yellowstone experience, back to her childhood. Dumb broad.

He'd about puked the night she'd raved on to him and Patty about that Yellowstone vacation. She'd loved having the whole family in one room, like some *Little House on the Prairie* fairy tale. Nobody had ever taken him on a pansy-ass vacation like that when he was a kid. Good thing, too, because he would have hated it. Only real reason for going out in the woods was to shoot yourself a bull elk.

His stomach began to pinch and he realized he'd better stop for some food. He started watching the billboards. Nothing but damned fast-food chains. He hated big business. Big business and big government, the scourge of the independent spirit in this country. Then he saw a small billboard for the Shooting Star Café. Falling Star was probably more like it—some poor guy trying to make ends meet while he shoveled most of his income to Uncle Sam. Mason decided to stop there and get something to go.

Even the star on the billboard needed some paint. They should have done it in that reflective gold. Maybe he'd suggest that when he got there. A little gold paint wouldn't cost much. Maybe...

Oh, shit. The gold star. The goddamned gold star on the pocket of that big cowboy in the café.

Swerving to the shoulder of the road, Fowler slammed on the brakes. Then he sat there cussing himself, that cowboy and his idiot sister-in-law. She'd been there, at the motel, all night long. The motel was out of rooms, the cowboy had said. He'd been sitting there at two in the morning, not using his. It had seemed weird at the time, but lots of things seemed weird at two in the morning.

Fowler slammed his fist against the steering wheel. That bitch was forever putting little gold stars on Josh for some stupid reason or other. Sure as the world that shit-kicking cowboy had given up his room to her and she'd rewarded him with a goddamned gold star. Fowler had sat there looking at the guy and for some reason that stupid little star on his pocket hadn't registered.

But it registered now. He looked for a break in traffic, cut across the highway, barreled the Land Rover through the weeds on the median and headed back the way he'd come. So the café owners had lied to him. He'd have to decide what to do about that, too. But first he had to find that little bitch and get his son. Nobody was going to stand in his way. Nobody.

JOSH WANTED a big snowman, taller than Shelby, so Boone decided Josh should have a snowman. Boone hadn't built all that many, himself, growing up as he had in Las Cruces, so he completely understood how Josh felt about making Frosty. Got snow, gotta have a snowman.

Shelby seemed to be having a good time, too, and Boone enjoyed watching her relax and play in the snow. He wondered if she'd noticed how many times they'd accidentally touched or brushed against each other during the snowman project.

Boone had sure noticed. The whole time they'd been working his mind had been filled with the thought of pushing her gently down in the snow and covering her body with his. He'd never been so obsessed with sex in his life.

Towards the end of the project, Eugene Sloan got into the act, coming out with an old battered hat and a carrot for the snowman's nose.

Making the head was Josh's job, and after Shelby helped him roll a snowball big enough, Boone lifted it on top. Then

Boone held Josh while he positioned stones for eyes and a mouth, the carrot for the nose, and crammed the hat over the snowman's head.

Eugene watched the final decorations with a smile on his narrow face. "Mighty fine work, folks."

From his perch in Boone's arms, Josh stared in fascination at the completed snowman. "Will he come alive now?" he asked hopefully.

"Hard to say," Boone replied. "I've heard sometimes that happens after dark. I'm afraid we won't be here to see that."

"I'll check it out for you, young man," Eugene said.

Josh nodded. "Good. 'Cause he might come alive. He gots a hat and that makes snowmens come alive."

"You folks have time for a cup of coffee or hot chocolate before you go?" Eugene asked. "On the house."

"Hot chocolate!" Josh bounced in Boone's arms. "Bob wants some, too!"

Boone thought of the miles they had yet to drive. He'd cleaned the snow off his truck, but they still needed to transfer Shelby and Josh's belongings into it. Sebastian was expecting him to roll in before nightfall, and they should leave soon in order to make it by then.

"We need to get a move on," he said, lowering Josh to the ground, "but why don't you give me your keys, Shelby? Then you and Josh can go on in and have something warm to drink while I load your stuff into the truck."

She glanced at him. "Why don't you give me *your* keys and I'll move everything while you and Josh go in and have something warm to drink."

Eugene laughed. "I can see a Mexican standoff coming. Let me take that boy in for some hot chocolate while you two get your loading done. Then Norma will fix you two coffees to go. How's that?"

Shelby smiled. "That would be wonderful, but I hate to put you to the trouble."

"No trouble. Helping folks out is what gets us out of bed of a morning."

"Well—"

"Can I, Shebby?" Josh tugged on her hand. "Can I, please?"

Boone understood Shelby's hesitation. He was a little reluctant to let Josh out of his sight, too. He still believed Mason could come back.

"All right," Shelby said finally. "We won't be long," she added, glancing at Eugene.

"Take your time." Eugene held his hand out to Josh. "Come on, son."

"Bob needs some, too."

"We'll make sure Bob gets some," Eugene said. "Let's go see if Norma has some marshmallows to put on top."

"Yum!" Josh hurried off, hand in hand with Eugene.

Shelby gazed after them, her expression uneasy.

Boone longed to wrap a comforting arm around her shoulders, but he didn't dare. "He'll be okay," he said.

"I'm sure he'll be fine." She sighed. "It's just that ever since the accident I've kept really close tabs on him. Preschool in the mornings has been the only time he's been out of my sight, and all the teachers there had strict instructions not to let anyone take him out of school for any reason."

"I'm sure Fowler's well down the road by now." Or so he hoped.

She turned to him, her blue eyes serious. "You're probably right. But let's not leave Josh in that café any longer than necessary."

"Go on in with him, Shelby. I can handle this."

She smiled. "Oh, no, you don't. Open up that big truck of

yours and I'll be there with our stuff before you know it."
She started toward the rental car.

"Oh, no, *you* don't." He fell into step beside her, his boots
crunching on the snow. "I'll help you carry. I'm betting that
the back seat is piled high."

"You'd win that bet. I wasn't sure how long we'd be gone,
so I threw in everything I could think of that Josh might
want. His whole toy box, practically. I hope you have
room."

"No problem. We can put some in the back of the king cab
with him and some in the camper." He held out his arms.
"Load me up."

Shelby laughed as she unlocked the back door of the
small sedan. "Gonna pull the big-strong-man routine, are
you?"

"A guy has to go with whatever works. Big-strong-man
works for me."

"You'll get no argument from me on that. I think big-
strong-man is what you do best."

They were flirting with each other, he thought, and they
both knew it. He shouldn't be doing that, and soon he'd
have to tell her why. He'd hoped to put it off for a while
longer, because he'd selfishly enjoyed the spark between
them.

She piled toys into his arms—trucks and cars of various
sizes, colorful boxes full of games and puzzles, and a whole
zoo of stuffed animals. In the process she kept bumping and
nudging him, and he didn't think it was accidental. He
longed to drop the whole pile and pull her into his arms. He
figured she wouldn't mind if he did.

His urges were getting out of hand, so he pretended interest in the toys. "Looks like this kid knows how to have fun."

"Materialistically, he's in good shape." She added more

toys to the pile. "My parents used to give me money, lots of money, and ask me to buy the Santa Claus presents."

Boone rested his chin on top of his stack to keep it from toppling. "A grandma who doesn't want to buy presents for a grandkid?" He couldn't picture such a thing. His mother had gone wild buying things for his nieces and nephews.

Shelby gathered an armload of things and kicked the door shut with her foot. "Past tense," she said tightly.

He closed his eyes. Damn. Well, that sure took care of the sexual tension in a hurry. "Sorry," he said.

"Hey, you can't be expected to remember." She started toward his truck. "Even I don't always remember. Ever since the accident, there are times I've been absolutely sure I'll wake up and it'll all be a bad dream."

Boone followed her. He felt helpless and inadequate because he couldn't think of anything to say or do that would ease her pain. In his experience, the only thing that worked at a time like this was simple human contact. More than anything else, Shelby needed to be held. And he was not the man for the job.

When they arrived at his truck, she rested her pile on the hood and turned to him. "Keys?"

Whoops. He should have taken his keys out of his pocket before she loaded him to the chin with toys. "They're, uh, in the right front pocket of my jeans." He felt the heat of a blush rising from his neck to his cheeks, but it was more from guilt than embarrassment. He wanted her to get those keys, wanted her hand sliding into his pocket. He was truly a pig.

She smiled and walked toward him, the teasing, flirty light back in her eyes. "If you were any other man, I'd say you engineered that on purpose."

"I swear I didn't." Not consciously, at least.

"I believe you. Hold still and I'll get the keys." She

walked behind him, which allowed her to shove her hand into his pocket the same way he would do it.

The process seemed to take forever. And although the sensation should have been exactly the same as if he'd been digging the keys out himself, it wasn't even close. And he was getting turned on. Very turned on.

"Got 'em." She stepped around in front of him and dangled the keys from her hand. "Now, wasn't that fun?"

His breath caught at the hunger in her eyes. If he tried to kiss her now, she wouldn't stop him. Oh, Lord. "Maybe a little too much fun," he said.

She gazed at him. "Boone, are you attracted to me?" she asked softly.

He swallowed and knew he had to come clean. Especially when she was looking at him like that, with eyes as clear and blue as a mountain lake. "Yep. Unfortunately."

"Unfortunately?" The sparkle faded from her eyes. "Is that because you'd rather not get involved with a woman in my crazy situation?"

"It's not your situation. It's mine."

Her eyes clouded. "Good grief. I should have guessed. You have a girlfriend."

"No, not exactly." He took a deep breath. "But I have...a baby girl."

Her jaw dropped.

He could imagine what she was thinking, and how her glorious picture of him had just shifted to something a lot less flattering. He hated having her think less of him, but truth was truth. "It's complicated. I just found out a few days ago, and I need...that is, I'm not sure what her mother will need..."

"Of course. You don't owe me any explanation whatsoever," she said quickly. "Forget I said anything. Your private life is none of my business." Avoiding his gaze, she held up the keys. "Which one?"

"The one with the round end." He felt completely miserable. "Listen, I do owe you an explanation after what happened last night. You probably think I'm some sex fiend."

"I most certainly do not." She unlocked the door and started fumbling with the catch that would release the front passenger seat and give him access to the back. "You're human, that's all. There's no crime in that. And you've been more than kind to Josh and me. How foolish of me to start imagining that you—oh, hell! Why can't I figure out this stupid seat?" And she started to cry.

To hell with whether he was the right guy to hold her or not. She needed a shoulder. "Move over," he said.

Turning, she leaned against the truck and covered her face with her hands. "Oh, God." Her body quivered with each muffled sob.

He dumped the armful of toys in the front seat, turned and coaxed her into his arms. "Come here, Shelby."

With a wail of despair she wrapped her arms around him and buried her face against the leather of his jacket.

He held her close, murmuring words of comfort as he stroked her back. Damn, she was tiny. The top of her head, even including the stocking cap she wore, only came to his breastbone. In order to kiss her he'd have to stand her on a box. Not that he intended to kiss her. He'd love to, but it wouldn't be right.

His job was to hold a frightened woman while she cried. She felt so small in his arms that he might have been comforting a kid. Except he knew better. Her breast had felt lush and full in his hand, her bottom nicely rounded and inviting against his groin. It was crazy, considering how different they were in size, but she fit more perfectly into his arms right now than any woman ever had. He could stand here holding her forever.

Slowly her sobs grew weaker and farther apart. At last she sniffed and rested quietly against him. "I don't suppose you have a handkerchief?"

"Sure." He continued to hold her close with one arm while he reached in his back pocket, pulled out a clean red bandanna and handed it to her.

She took it with a watery chuckle. "This is too perfect. The cowboy who saved me at Yellowstone gave me a red bandanna, too." She blew her nose.

Instantly he was jealous. "What cowboy?"

"When I was seven and on a family vacation, I got lost, and this cowboy was out riding and found me. That probably explains why I have this thing for cowboys."

"Oh." So he was only a generic attraction. His grip on her loosened.

In contrast, hers tightened up. "That came out wrong." She gazed up at him, her nose red and her eyelashes still spiked with tears. "I might have noticed you because you're a cowboy, but now that I know you as a person, I like you because of who you are, not what you are." She managed a smile. "Thank you for letting me get your leather jacket all wet. You're the best, Boone."

He was still stuck back on her earlier comment. "Do you go out with a lot of cowboys, then?"

She looked confused. "Why would you think that?"

"You said you had a *thing* for cowboys."

"Oh." She toyed with a button on his jacket. "That sounds really bad, doesn't it? Like I hang out at country-western bars and pick up anything in a Stetson. The truth is, I haven't gone out, period, not since Josh was born, and I've never dated a cowboy. It's just that you showed up right when I was in trouble, sort of like in Yellowstone when I was seven and that other cowboy showed up. It made me realize I've always sort of..." She glanced away, her cheeks turning rosy. "Never mind. I talk too much. We need to get the truck loaded." She tried to step back.

He held her captive. "Tell me."

"It's silly. And it has nothing to do with you."

"Tell me anyway." How he loved holding her. Absolutely loved it.

"Okay, but I'm warning you, it'll sound dumb." She took a deep breath and looked up at him again. "I think, subconsciously, I've been wishing my cowboy would come along some day, and sweep me off my feet. Like some girls dream about their Prince Charming. I realize after meeting you that I've been dreaming about my cowboy, who would lift me up to his saddle and we'd ride off into the sunset together. I even wonder if I was headed up to Yellowstone to find him. Well, not him, exactly. He'd be older than dirt by now. But someone like him. Stupid, huh?"

He gazed down at her, a lump in his throat. If he didn't have a baby and obligations waiting for him at the Rocking D, he would kiss Shelby this very minute. He wouldn't need a box. She was so light he'd be able to lift her up. She could wrap her legs around his hips and they could kiss all day like that. And he would sweep her away.

Shelby nodded. "Don't worry, you won't hurt my feelings if you think that's a juvenile fantasy. I know it's not very adult to still believe in fairy tales. I'm working on that."

"No." He shook his head. "Don't work on it. Don't change yourself, Shelby. It's a good dream."

"But it's still just a dream," she said. "I need to focus on reality at the moment."

"I wish you didn't have to. Damn it, I wish I could be your—"

She laid a finger against his lips, silencing him. "It's okay," she whispered.

This time, when she stepped out of his arms, he let her go.

7

MASON WAS at a disadvantage trying to watch oncoming traffic for a glimpse of Shelby and Josh, and he hated being at a disadvantage. There was a good chance he'd pass them without knowing it in the split second he'd have to figure out who was in each car. And he felt like a fool for believing the story he'd been fed. He was usually more suspicious of people than that, but those local yokels hadn't seemed smart enough to trick anybody.

When he'd nearly reached the motel without spotting them, he decided he'd have to start his search by getting some straight information from that lying little motel owner about what kind of car the bitch was driving and exactly when she'd left the motel. The scrawny little guy and his overweight wife should be easy enough to intimidate. After all, they were pretty isolated on this lonely stretch of road.

First he'd cruise past the place, though, and get the lay of the land. With luck, no other customers would be around to interfere with the questioning process. If the motel owner knew what was good for him, he'd cooperate. Mason was so damned hungry his stomach hurt. That, on top of being lied to, had put him in a really bad mood.

The first thing he saw as he drove past the place was a big old king cab sitting in the café parking lot. He vaguely remembered it had been there when he'd left. The second thing he saw nearly made him swerve off the road. That dumb-ass cowboy was standing beside the truck, and unless Mason missed his guess, the little lady in his arms was Shelby.

His heart beat faster. Yep, it was her, all right. He'd seen her in that ski jacket a few times. The two of them seemed oblivious to the world. So *that's* how things were.

She must be mighty grateful to that cowboy. Mason could just imagine how she'd shown her gratitude. He ground his teeth together. Patricia had been a runaround like that, too, ready to trade her sexual favors for whatever she wanted. He'd never trusted her around other guys, not from day one. Well, she'd got what she deserved, and now he intended to get what he deserved.

Josh was nowhere in sight, and Mason wondered if there was any chance he could snatch the kid while these two were pawing each other. Obviously he needed to do a little reconnaissance work.

He continued south until the road curved to the right and he could no longer see the motel in his rearview mirror. Parking carefully on the snowy shoulder, he left the motor running and grabbed his binoculars. The large snowbanks left by the plows gave him good cover while he hiked back to where he could see the motel parking lot.

Damned snow might as well be good for something. In fact, a snowdrift made a perfect bunker, hiding him from passing cars as he crouched down and peered through his binoculars.

What a charming couple. Made him want to hurl, just watching them. He searched the area for Josh and saw no sign of the little brat. But he was somewhere around, sure as the world, probably pestering the café owner for candy or cookies. Mason had that covered. He'd stowed a ton of candy in the Land Rover. Candy was cheap and it usually worked to keep the kid quiet.

The cowboy and Shelby managed to tear themselves

away from each other, and Mason watched closely, trying to figure out what was going on. When he realized what they were doing as they loaded things into the big truck, he cursed a blue streak. Damned cowboy was *taking her with him.*

Mason's plan was shot to hell. He could do fine against the bitch, but the cowboy put a whole new spin on things. The guy might be dumb as a post, but he was big. He probably thought of himself as some frigging Sir Galahad, ready to defend Shelby to the death.

The courts would excuse a man for pushing around the woman who'd kidnapped his son. But with the cowboy around, that wouldn't be easy, and although Mason could always use his .45 Magnum to take the big guy out, he'd have a tough time making it look like self-defense.

Maybe, if he studied the situation, he could engineer another accident to get rid of both Shelby and this John Wayne type. He probably couldn't top the genius of that boating accident, though. Even Shelby, who hated his guts, didn't suspect a thing. That had been one slick operation.

Mason kept his binoculars pointed toward the café, and eventually the scrawny motel owner and his fat wife appeared with Josh. A sickening farewell party followed— hugs all around, until it pained Mason to watch them slobber all over each other. That was one thing he'd liked about Patricia's old man and old lady, besides the obvious advantage that they'd been filthy rich. They hadn't gone in for all this hugging shit. To Mason's way of thinking, a hug was wasted energy unless it counted as foreplay. He'd hug a babe any day of the week if she looked like she'd put out.

Finally the cowboy buckled Josh into the back seat and helped Shelby into the front. Couldn't let her climb in. Oh, no, he had to get his hands on her and lift her in. Mason swore eloquently. He'd bet the farm those two had been doing the horizontal hula while he'd been crammed into a hard plastic booth trying to get some shut-eye. Somebody would have to pay for that.

Unfortunately it wouldn't be the café owner and his wife. Mason didn't have time to play with them now. Maybe another trip. Right now he had to get his butt back to the Land Rover and follow that truck to wherever it was going.

The happy little threesome would never guess he was behind them, either. Patricia never had, in all the times he'd followed her back when she'd pretended to be his ever-faithful wife. Too bad he'd never caught her with one of her lovers, or the divorce settlement would have looked a hell of a lot different. Yeah, he'd been shafted then, but he'd even the score this time. All he had to do was get that kid of his and he'd be on Easy Street.

"WHEN WE GONNA get there?"

"Oh, Josh." Shelby groaned as the question that had been asked at least a hundred times in the four hours they'd been on the road came sailing up from the back seat yet again.

"Not too much longer," Boone said. His calm tone betrayed no irritation whatsoever. He acted as if Josh's query was brand-new, interesting and worthy of a reasonable answer. "Maybe a couple of hours. Maybe less, depending on the road conditions."

Shelby had decided Boone Connor was a saint. Nothing else explained his incredible patience with a squirmy three-year-old who'd talked nonstop, it seemed, from the time they'd left the café.

"How long's *that?*" Josh asked.

"Plenty of time for a little nap," Shelby suggested hopefully.

"Naps are for babies," Josh said. "I'm a big boy. Me and

Bob, we're gonna ride horsies when we get there. Right, Boone?"

"Tomorrow morning," Boone said. "Don't forget it'll be almost dark when we get there tonight."

"And my snowman could be comin' alive."

"Could be."

"Is Mr. Sloan gonna call us if he comes alive?"

"He might."

"Me and Bob, we can ride horsies in the dark. We gots flashlights."

"Ah, but the horses will be sleeping," Boone said. "All tucked into their warm stalls for the night. You wouldn't want to wake them up, would you?"

"No," Josh said. "But can we see 'em sleeping? Me and Bob, we'd be very, very, very, very quiet." He started whispering. *"Very, very, very quiet."*

"Then maybe we can go down to the barn," Boone said.

"Yay! Yay, yay, yay!" Josh started singing. "We're going to the ba-arn, we're going to the ba-arn, and see the horsies slee-ping." Then he paused. "Now how long is it?"

Shelby sighed. "How about if I read you another book?"

"Nope."

"We'll count cars," Boone said. "And see who wins. I'll take red. Shelby, what color do you want?"

"Green." She flashed him a grateful smile. She'd only taken one car trip with her family, and she wasn't very experienced at coming up with games to play on the road, but Boone seemed to know exactly how to handle Josh's boredom.

"I want black!" Josh said. "Like Batman gots!"

"Oh, how about yellow, Josh?" Shelby said. "You like yellow, don't you?" Although it was silly of her, she'd rather not have Josh pointing out all the black cars on the road. Mason's Land Rover was black, and even though Shelby was convinced he was far away, black vehicles still gave her the willies. She'd rather not have Josh sing out every time he saw one.

"I want black," Josh insisted.

"Then black it is," Shelby said, not wanting to argue about it.

The game was a success, giving Josh a chance to show his hero Boone that he knew his colors and his numbers. Shelby and Josh were tied at six each, with Boone trailing with four.

"Seven!" Josh shouted.

"Where?" A chill went down Shelby's spine as it had each time Josh had pointed out a car, until she was able to see it and make sure it wasn't a Land Rover. She craned her neck. "I don't see a black car."

"I seed it. Seven."

"I don't see it, either, buddy," Boone said. "Was it going the other way?"

"It was up there." Josh pointed up toward Boone's rear-view mirror.

Shelby had a sick feeling in the pit of her stomach as she turned and looked back down the road behind them. "I still don't see it."

"It's gone," Josh said. "But it counts, right?"

"Sure, it counts." Shelby continued with the game, but she kept glancing in the rearview mirror, looking for that black car Josh had seen. She pictured a big Cadillac driven by a retired couple who were cruising along under the speed limit. Or an old junker limping down the road as best it could. Anything but a Land Rover.

Eventually she realized Josh had stopped counting the cars. She glanced back and saw that he'd fallen asleep. "He's finally conked out," she murmured to Boone. "You've been extremely tolerant."

Boone smiled. "He's just a normal kid. That's kind of amazing, all things considered."

"I know. I give thanks every day that he hasn't been warped by what he's been through."

"I'll bet you're the one who can take credit for that, Shelby."

She shrugged. "I think it's Josh. He was born with a sunny disposition, and even if life knocks him down, he smiles and gets right back up." She clenched her hands together in her lap. "At least he has so far. If Mason gets ahold of him, I'm not sure how long that resiliency will last."

"You were worried about that mysterious black car Josh saw, weren't you?"

"Yeah." She took a deep breath and blew it out. "Mason drives a black Land Rover."

"I know. Eugene told me."

Shelby felt an overwhelming attack of conscience. "Boone, you have no business getting involved in this. I should never have agreed to it. What if Mason isn't on his way up to Wyoming? What if he somehow figured out what we've done, and that was his Land Rover Josh saw in the rearview mirror?"

"All the more reason for you to be with me."

"But don't you see?" Shelby gazed at the determined clench of Boone's jaw. He was too noble for his own good. "You don't deserve to be sucked into whatever scenario Mason has in mind. He's a violent man, and I don't know what he might do. You shouldn't put yourself in harm's way for somebody you don't even know."

He sent her a long look. "The fact is, I would do the same for a stranger. But I don't think of you as a stranger. Maybe that's how you think of me, though."

"No. No, I don't." She gazed back at him, instantly filled with remorse. She'd hurt his feelings, which was the last thing on earth she wanted to do. "I think of you as a friend," she said. "An incredibly generous friend. And that's why I'm concerned about you getting involved. I'm not in the habit of dragging my friends into nasty situations. I really thought Mason would head down the road to Wyoming and you'd never have to deal with him. Now I'm not so sure."

"Just concentrate on Josh," Boone said gently. "Do what's best for that little boy, and you'll be making the right decision."

She had no doubt that meant sticking close to Boone. "Even if I impose horribly on you in the process?"

"I'll let you know if you're imposing on me," he said. "So far you're not even close."

"You're too good." She shook her head in wonder. "You must have been raised in a warm and loving family, to have such a generous heart."

"Warm and loving, so long as my dad was sober. If he was drunk, all hell broke lose and the smart ones ducked for cover."

Shelby took a moment to digest that information. Somehow she'd imagined Boone with a golden childhood, light years away from her cold and isolated upbringing. "That must have been rough, growing up like that," she said softly.

He grimaced. "Sometimes. And you'd think I'd have learned how the bottle changes a man. But no, I had to get myself plastered and prove I could be an idiot under the influence, too."

"Oh, Boone, I can't picture you doing anything bad, drunk or sober."

"How about having sex and not using any protection?"

"People get carried away sometimes." The thought of Boone getting carried away thrilled her to her toes. "I can imagine how that might happen. You're so—" She stopped herself before she said something really embarrassing.

"I'm lower than a snake, is what I am. Jessica was only trying to be kind to me, and I repaid her by making her pregnant. I don't blame her for not telling me once she found out. She probably wasn't sure she wanted me around the baby."

Shelby laid her hand on Boone's arm. He was trembling. "Listen, I don't know this woman or her thought processes, but I do know you. I would trust you with any child, of any age. She should, too."

"Then why did she name Sebastian and Travis as godfathers?" He gripped the steering wheel so hard his knuckles grew white. "Because she wanted them to keep an eye on me when she couldn't be there to do it, that's why."

"She's not at the ranch?"

"Not right now."

"Where is she?" Shelby was woman enough to admit being relieved that Jessica wouldn't be there when they arrived. She'd been bracing herself for meeting the woman who had carried Boone's child. She hadn't been looking forward to it.

"She has some sort of problem, and she didn't want the baby to be part of it. She dropped Elizabeth off at the Rocking D two months ago."

"*Two months?* How old is this baby?"

"She'd be four months now, going on five."

"She hasn't seen her baby in more than two months?" Even Patricia wouldn't have pulled something like that, Shelby thought, and Patricia had definitely foisted Josh on Shelby at every opportunity.

"No, but she calls every once in awhile, Sebastian said. Short calls, asking if Elizabeth's okay. Something must have really scared her and made her think the baby would be in danger if they stuck together."

"Well, that I can understand." Thinking back, Shelby now realized that some of Patricia's "neglect" might have been a way to keep Josh out of harm's way. But not all of it. Patricia had once admitted Mason tricked her into getting pregnant to get another hold over her. She'd never really wanted a child.

"Sebastian and Travis have hired a private detective to find Jessica," Boone said. "When we get there I'm going to take over that expense and do whatever else I can."

"I'm amazed you didn't hightail it up there two months ago."

"I would have. Jessica wrote letters asking all three of us—me, Sebastian and Travis—to be Elizabeth's godfathers, but my letter got delayed."

"Wait a minute." Shelby was having a hard time sorting this out. "She didn't specifically name you as the father?"

"No, but I know it's me, even if I don't remember exactly what happened that night."

Shelby gazed at him. "You mean you don't remember...the, um, act itself?"

A ruddy stain crept up his neck. "Nope. And that's pitiful. Shows you what drink can do to a man."

"Well, I don't have a lot of experience in this area, but I always thought that the more a man drank, the less he could...perform, so to speak."

"But I'm Irish."

Shelby laughed. "Sorry," she said, quickly composing herself. "I know this isn't a laughing matter. But I don't see what being Irish has to do with it."

"An Irishman can do anything drunk that he can do sober. He just might not remember it afterwards."

"I see." Shelby couldn't help smiling at Boone's sturdy

belief in his inherited abilities. She could see that arguing with him wouldn't do any good, but she also wondered if he was truly this baby's father. Her heart grew a little lighter with the knowledge that he might not be.

"At any rate, don't go thinking I'm doing all this for you and Josh. I'm doing it for me, too."

"How do you figure?"

He glanced her way, and his green eyes were troubled. "By helping you, I can try to convince myself I'm not such a bad guy, after all."

"Boone." She squeezed his arm. Touching him gave her such pleasure that she felt guilty using comfort as an excuse. "You are not a bad guy. You are so not a bad guy."

"Thanks, Shelby." He sighed. "All I know is, I have to do right by Jessica, if she can forgive me, and that little baby of mine."

"I'm sure you will." Shelby longed to ask Boone exactly what he meant by that, but she didn't want to pry into something that was really none of her business. Still, she might make it her business, if she could determine one critical point in this situation. The most important thing about Jessica, from Shelby's viewpoint, was whether or not Boone was in love with her.

8

THE CLOSER Boone got to the Rocking D, the more his thoughts seemed like a bed of hot coals. One concern would flare up and he'd worry about that for a while until another one began to flicker and glow, drawing his attention. For one thing, he worried about whether Elizabeth would like the set of blocks he'd brought her. He would have rather made his own set, but he hadn't had the time.

Then he worried about whether Elizabeth would like *him*. She'd had more than two months to get used to Sebastian. As for Travis—well, Travis would have won her over in five minutes. Travis had a gift that way. But Boone was afraid he'd scare her with his size and his big hands.

When Boone wasn't thinking about Elizabeth and how that mess would turn out, he worried about whether he could keep Josh from ending up with Mason Fowler. He was as committed to that cause now as Shelby.

Like Shelby, he had an uneasy suspicion that Fowler might be tailing them. Boone had spent a fair share of time checking the rearview mirror, but he hadn't noticed a black Land Rover. A couple of times while going up a hill he'd thought maybe a vehicle behind them could have been the Land Rover, but it had been too far away to be sure, and he hadn't wanted to worry Shelby.

Taking her and Josh to the Rocking D was the one thing Boone was positive about, the one thing that didn't worry him at all. From the Rocking D, with Sebastian and Travis as potential backups, Boone believed he had his best chance to defend the woman and the boy. Out here on the road wasn't a good place to make a stand.

Fowler struck him as a survivalist type who might have practiced the art of following a vehicle without being seen. The guy probably had more than one gun and maybe even an assault rifle. But if he needed to have custody of Josh in order to get any money, he wouldn't be mowing anybody down with his firepower.

He might have wanted Shelby to run. Boone had thought about that some, too, after Shelby had mentioned the possibility. Fowler might have decided that in order to cinch his chances of getting the kid, he had to make Shelby look bad. So he'd scared her into taking off. Then he could look like a frantic father if he chased her down and took his kid back.

But he hadn't counted on Boone.

Shelby would be safe from Mason at the Rocking D. Boone hoped she'd be safe from him. The thought of making love to her never left his mind for long. Riding in the truck together for most of the day hadn't helped. But they wouldn't have much opportunity to be alone with so many people around the ranch. He was counting on that to keep him honest.

"It's black as pitch out here," Shelby said as they traveled down the dirt road that led to the turnoff to the ranch. "How do you know where you're going?"

"Habit," Boone said. He kept his voice low so he wouldn't wake Josh, who was still asleep in his car seat. "I've based my horseshoeing operation at the Rocking D every summer for the past nine years."

"So that's how long you've known your friend, the one who owns the ranch?"

"Yep." He loved Shelby's voice. It had a musical sound to

it, and her slight Texas accent made her sound sexy, no matter what she said.

"How'd you meet him?" she asked.

"I came to the ranch drumming up business. I was living out of my camper, and Sebastian and his wife were scraping by at the time. Sebastian offered me a place to stay if I'd cut him a deal on the shoes every year. That's how it started."

"Wait a minute. Didn't you tell me Sebastian's a newly-wed?"

"Yeah. He and his first wife got a divorce about three years back. He just married his neighbor, Matty."

"Okay. Sebastian and Matty." Shelby paused as if committing the names to memory. "What do they look like?"

"Matty's small and blond, like you." *But not stacked like you are*, he thought, but decided that wouldn't be a good thing to mention. "She's the no-nonsense type. Can rope and ride as well as a man. Sebastian's hair is...brown, I guess. He's built pretty solid, but he's not as tall as me."

"Got it," Shelby said. "And what about your other friend? What does he do?"

"Travis? He used to be Matty's head wrangler, but now he works for both Matty and Sebastian, I guess."

"Didn't you say he was getting married tomorrow?"

"Yeah." Boone chuckled. "Never thought I'd see the day, either. He's quite a lady's man. Good dancer, quick with a joke. He used to walk around saying, 'So many women, so little time.' But according to Sebastian, he really fell hard for Gwen Hawthorne." Boone hadn't considered it before, but he was glad Travis had a woman. That way he wouldn't make a play for Shelby.

"And what does Gwen look like?"

"Near as I remember, she's tall with dark hair. Looks sort of like an Indian princess. I think maybe there's some Cheyenne in her background. She runs a bed-and-breakfast in Huerfano."

"That little town we just went through, right?"

"Yep."

"I liked it," Shelby said. "The way people are fixing up those turn-of-the-century houses is nice."

"Gwen's place, Hawthorne House, is one of those. Skiing and tourism saved Huerfano," Boone said. "Used to be a booming mining town, but the mines played out. The ranches around here couldn't keep a town going, but tourists can."

"I've never thought of living in a small town before, but if I get custody of Josh—"

"You mean *when* you get custody of Josh," Boone said. Any other possibility would be obscene.

"Okay, *when* I get custody of Josh." She sighed and leaned her head against the seat. "You have no idea what it means to me, having you on my side, Boone. I haven't felt as if I had anybody on my side ever since the accident."

He glanced over at her. In the faint light from the dash she looked beautiful, but pale and vulnerable, too. She needed him, and how he longed to be everything she needed, in every way. But he couldn't. "Don't you have a lawyer?"

"Yeah, my parents' lawyer. He loves to paint the 'worst case scenario' as he puts it, which involves Mason winning full custody and me only getting limited visiting rights. He seems to relish reminding me that judges are usually fathers and will quite possibly side with Mason in this case. My parents picked a real crepe hanger for a lawyer. He's a cold fish, just like they—" She turned to him, her eyes wide. "Forget I said that. My God, they just *died*. I have no right to—"

"Sure you do," he said gently. He reached over and took her hand, thinking that any person would do the same. Taking her hand wasn't a sexual thing. The problem was that once he had her hand in his, he wanted to bring it to his lips. He wanted to pull the truck over to the side of the road and kiss her. Really kiss her.

But he didn't.

"My parents didn't know any better." Shelby held tight to his hand. "Somebody, maybe my grandparents, taught them that money and prestige were everything. They taught Patricia the same thing."

"But not you." He rubbed a thumb over the delicate bones in the back of her hand and wondered if a big guy like him could make love to her without doing damage. Of course, he'd never find out.

"I've always been the different one in the family," Shelby said. "I never quite fitted in, never liked getting all dressed up and going to fancy parties, never wanted a career in the limelight. Maybe that was because I wasn't the pretty one, but—"

"Are you crazy?"

She turned toward him. "You mean because I blew a chance to be part of high society?"

"Not that! You just said you weren't the pretty one! You're—" He suddenly realized he'd gotten loud and was about to tell her she was beautiful, gorgeous, sexy. "You're very pretty," he said quietly, grateful for the darkened interior of the truck so she wouldn't see the hunger in his eyes.

"Shebby's *bootiful*," Josh said from the back seat.

"Listen to the kid," Boone murmured, wishing he could speak as freely as the three-year-old about his feelings for Shelby. "He knows what he's talking about."

"You're both embarrassing me." She eased her hand out of Boone's grasp.

The minute Shelby took her hand from his, Boone felt disconnected from an important energy source. He longed to feel that power surge again, and he had to stop himself from reclaiming her hand. Uh-oh. He was starting to need Shelby McFarland.

Shelby turned toward the back seat. "How long have you been awake back there?"

"I dunno. I heared you talking. When are we gonna get there? Me and Bob, we gots to go potty."

Boone spotted the entrance to the ranch looming up ahead. "How about if we're almost there? How's that?"

"We're there? Really there?"

"See those two poles with another pole across the top?" Boone asked.

"Yep!"

"That's the main gate. There's a sign hanging down from the top pole. You might not be able to read it in the dark, but it says Rocking D Ranch, and it has Sebastian's brand on either side."

"Brand? What's that?"

"His special sign. He stamps it on all the cows that he owns, and on a few other things around the ranch, too." Boone decided not to get into the details of branding cows. Truth be told, Boone had never much liked the process, himself, which was why he was a blacksmith and not a cattleman.

"What's it look like?" Josh asked.

"It's a letter D sitting sideways on top of a curved line, like the rocker on a rocking chair. The whole thing looks kind of like a cradle."

Josh thought about that for a while. "I know my ABCs," he announced. "Wanna hear?"

"Sure." Boone welcomed the distraction. Up ahead was Elizabeth, his little baby girl. His stomach clenched.

Josh began to sing the alphabet song, but he only got to

the letter M before he interrupted himself. "Lights!" he chortled. "I see a house!"

Shelby let out a long breath. "Oh, Boone, what a lovely place. You didn't tell me it was made of peeled logs. And a stone chimney with smoke coming out. Could anything be more welcoming?"

"It's a nice house," Boone said as he parked behind Travis's shiny black rig. He was so nervous he thought he might be sick. Thank God he had Shelby and Josh with him. They helped calm him down a little.

"It's a *great* house," Josh said.

Boone unbuckled his seat belt. "Sebastian planted those aspens in the front." He noticed the aspens were taller than last year. He'd missed this place, but the rush of homecoming he always felt was overshadowed by a bad case of nerves. "You can't see the mountains too well when it's this dark, but Sebastian gets a real pretty view from here."

"I can see them," Shelby said. "Just barely."

"Me, too!" Josh exclaimed.

"I can hardly wait for morning," Shelby added, "so I can see everything better. Josh, this is a little bit like Yellowstone, with the mountains and the trees and everything."

"Do you gots geezers?" Josh asked.

"No, afraid not." Boone smiled, despite his nervousness. "But you could ask Sebastian about it. Tell him you're looking for geezers." Boone liked to kid Sebastian about his age. He'd just turned thirty-five, which made him the oldest of the bunch, and nobody ever let him forget it, either.

"Where's the horsies?" Josh asked.

"Down in the barn." Boone opened his door and drew in a lungful of cool, clean air scented with pine. "We'll go take a look in a little while, after you go potty and get some chow into you."

"Can't we see 'em *now*? Bob wants to see 'em now."

"No, Josh," Shelby said. "It wouldn't be polite to rush down there. We need to go in and meet Boone's friends first."

Boone rounded the truck and helped Shelby down. He wished he could just hold on to her for a little while. He knew holding Shelby would steady him.

She rested her hands on his arms. "Are you okay?"

"Sure."

"But you're shaking."

"Nervous about the baby, I guess."

She squeezed his arms. "It'll be fine, Boone. I—"

"Gots to go *pot-ty*," Josh sang out from the back seat.

"Let's get him out," Boone said. He'd barely lifted the little boy to the ground when a commotion came from the house. He turned as people and dogs erupted out of the front door. They surged across the porch and down the steps toward Boone's truck.

"They gots doggies, too!" Josh cried in delight.

"Big doggies," Shelby said as she scooped Josh up in her arms.

"Hey, Boone!" Sebastian was in the lead, a huge smile on his face. "Where you been, boy? Can't believe a little snow would slow you down!"

"I tried to talk my way through it." Boone clasped Sebastian's hand as Fleafarm, Sebastian's mixed breed, and Sadie, Matty's Great Dane, danced happily around him, panting and barking.

Boone's glance moved to Matty close on Sebastian's heels, and Travis and Gwen calling out greetings as they brought up the rear. Nobody was holding a baby. Elizabeth must be taking a nap or something. He was relieved. He'd have a little more time to prepare himself.

"I'd like you all to meet Shelby McFarland," Boone said. He quite naturally put an arm around her shoulders to guide her forward and it sure felt right, as if he was bringing his sweetheart home to meet his friends. Which of course he wasn't, and he'd do well to remember that. "And this here's Josh," he added.

"Pleased to meet you," Sebastian said, his smile wide but his gaze assessing.

"Thank you for having us on such short notice and in the midst of all your activities," Shelby said.

"Wouldn't have it any other way," Sebastian said. Then he glanced back over his shoulder. "Matty? There you are." He scooped her in next to him. "This is my wife, Matty," he said with obvious pride.

"Welcome to the Rocking D, Josh and Shelby," Matty said. Her smile was as bright as her husband's, but she gave Shelby and Josh the once-over, too. Then she glanced at Boone. "Do I get a hug, big guy?"

"You bet." Boone embraced her warmly. "Congratulations, Matty. Wish I'd been here for the ceremony."

"Yeah, yeah, yeah. Break it up, break it up." Travis appeared and clapped Boone on the shoulder. "At least you're here for mine." He tipped his Stetson in Shelby's direction. "Though I can see why you might want to dawdle and keep this beautiful woman to yourself. Pleased to meet you, Shelby. You, too, Josh." He caught Gwen by the hand and pulled her close. "You remember this lovely lady, right, Boone?"

"Sure do." Boone touched the brim of his hat. "Good to see you, Gwen. And this here's Shelby and Josh."

"I'm glad to meet both of you," Gwen said. Her expression was friendly, but as openly curious as Matty and Sebastian's had been. "How was your trip?"

"Good, thanks to Boone," Shelby said, glancing at him. "He kept Josh entertained the whole way."

"We counted cars," Josh said. "And I winned. But now me and Bob gots to go potty."

"I'll bet you do." Matty stepped forward and put her arm around Shelby. "Let's get you both inside," she said, guiding them toward the porch. "The guys can bring the stuff in."

"You're probably both starving, too." Gwen fell into step on the other side of Shelby and the dogs pranced at her heels. "And you might even be able to use a glass of wine, Shelby."

"Sounds wonderful," Shelby said.

"You gots lemonade?" Josh asked.

"I think we can find some," Matty said.

Boone watched them hustle Shelby and Josh into the house and felt displaced. He was glad they'd welcomed them into the group and were taking such good care of them, but damn it, he'd gotten used to the job.

"Who's Bob?" Sebastian glanced around the yard.

"Josh's imaginary friend," Boone said, gazing after them. "The way Josh talks, you'd think he really existed. We always have to make sure we include Bob in everything."

"*We?*" Travis asked. "Sounds cozy."

Boone whipped around to face him and knew he was blushing. "I didn't mean it like that. It's just that we've all been together since last night, and I—"

"Easy, big fella." Sebastian rested a hand on Boone's shoulder. "She's a nice girl. I can see why you're interested."

"I'm *not* interested. I'm only helping her out!"

"That's not the way it looks from where I'm standing," Travis said. "I say you're interested. And so's she."

"That's ridiculous," Boone said. "I can't be interested, and you know it."

"I do? What, you took a vow of celibacy I don't know about?"

"Yeah," Sebastian said. "Darlene's out of the picture, so why can't you be interested?"

Boone stared at both of them. "Don't be dense. Because of Jessica. And the baby."

Sebastian and Travis exchanged a look. Then Sebastian turned to Boone. "You're not assuming you're Elizabeth's father, are you?"

"Of course I'm assuming it. Which means I have an obligation to Jessica."

Travis laughed and shook his head. "I can't believe this."

"It's not funny!"

Sebastian grinned. "Yeah, it is. Travis and I have dealt with the same damned thing you're putting yourself through. Both of us almost missed a chance for happiness with the women we love because we convinced ourselves we had an obligation to Jessica."

Boone squared his shoulders. "In the first place, I'm not even close to being in love with Shelby." He felt a twinge of guilt. He was lying to his two best friends. "Second of all, you don't have an obligation to Jessica, because you're not the baby's father. But I am, so I do."

Travis sighed and glanced at Sebastian. "Well, maybe he's going to have to find out the hard way, like we did. It'd be nice to think a man was willing to take his best friends' advice, but that's obviously not the case. I think we're flapping our gums for nothing, Sebastian."

"Could be."

"Look, you two, there is nothing going on between Shelby and me," Boone said. Another twinge of guilt.

"Oh, there is most definitely something going on," Sebastian said. "The question is whether you're going to be smart enough to take advantage of the fact. Come on, let's get your gear out of the truck, or my chicken dinner is going to be overcooked before we're ready to eat it."

9

THE INSIDE of the ranch house was so cozy, Shelby sighed with delight. Matty took their coats and directed them to the bathroom down the hall. Then she and Gwen left to organize drinks for everyone, including wine for Shelby and lemonade for Josh.

On her way through the living room, Shelby took appreciative notice of everything. The furniture was the kind that could withstand dogs and children and big men wearing dusty jeans. A wing chair and an old rocker flanked a wear-polished leather sofa, and a sturdy wooden coffee table sat in front of it.

The house not only looked comfortable, it smelled that way, too—a homey combination of cedar crackling in the fireplace, chicken in the oven and sweet peas in a jug on the coffee table.

So this is what a real home feels like. Shelby contrasted it with her parents' showplace in San Antonio. After growing up in a formal atmosphere, Shelby had known what she didn't want. Seeing this rustic, comfortable room, she finally knew what she did want.

A light was on in a bedroom at the end of the hall, and Shelby heard a baby coo, followed by the low murmur of a woman's voice. Shelby's stomach rolled. *Jessica.*

She hustled Josh into the bathroom, flipped on the light and closed the door. Then she leaned against it and fought for breath. Suddenly this perfect house wasn't so perfect

Here's a **HOT** offer for you!

Get set for a sizzling summer read...

with **2 FREE ROMANCE BOOKS**
and a **FREE MYSTERY GIFT!**

NO CATCH! NO OBLIGATION TO BUY!

Simply complete and return this card and you'll get **2 FREE BOOKS** and **A FREE GIFT** – yours to keep!

Visit us online at
www.eHarlequin.com

🌀 The first shipment is yours to keep, **absolutely free!**

🌀 Enjoy the convenience of Harlequin Temptation® books delivered right to your door, before they're available in stores!

🌀 Take advantage of special low pricing for **Reader Service Members only!**

🌀 After receiving your free books we hope you'll want to remain a subscriber. But the choice is always yours—to continue or cancel, any time at all! So why not take us up on this fabulous invitation, with no risk of any kind. You'll be glad you did!

342 HDL C26G

142 HDL C256
(H-T-OS-06/00)

◀ DETACH HERE AND MAIL CARD TODAY! ▼

Name: _____
(Please Print)

Address: _____ Apt.#: _____

City: _____

State/Prov.: _____ Zip/Postal Code: _____

Offer limited to one per household and not valid to current Harlequin Temptation® subscribers. All orders subject to approval. © 1998 HARLEQUIN ENTERPRISES LTD. ® & ™ are trademarks owned by Harlequin Enterprises Ltd.

The Harlequin Reader Service® —Here's how it works:

Accepting your 2 free books and gift places you under no obligation to buy anything. You may keep the books and gift and return the shipping statement marked "cancel." If you do not cancel, about a month later we'll send you 4 additional novels and bill you just $3.34 each in the U.S., or $3.80 each in Canada, plus 25¢ delivery per book and applicable taxes if any.* That's the complete price and — compared to cover prices of $3.99 each in the U.S. and $4.50 each in Canada — it's quite a bargain! You may cancel at any time, but if you choose to continue, every month we'll send you 4 more books, which you may either purchase at the discount price or return to us and cancel your subscription.

*Terms and prices subject to change without the notice. Sales tax applicable in N.Y. Canadian residents will be charged applicable provincial taxes and GST.

anymore. She felt like crying. For a few precious minutes she'd imagined herself fitting into this world of Boone's, and she'd loved the feeling. But if Jessica had arrived, that could only mean one thing. She was here to see Boone. And Boone would have no more time for Shelby.

"Shebby?" Josh stared up at her.

She gazed down at the little boy and quickly whipped her priorities into order. This whole trip wasn't about her, it was about Josh. If Boone stopped paying attention to him because of Jessica and the baby, he'd be devastated. She'd have to be ready to compensate, as she always had.

"You look like you been runnin'," Josh said.

"It's the altitude," she said, taking a deep breath.

"You gots a bad altitude?"

She couldn't help smiling. "*Al*titude," she said. "That means we're up in the mountains, which is a higher altitude than down in San Antonio. There's less oxygen up here, so that sometimes makes it a little harder to catch your breath."

"What's ox-gin?"

"Something in the air that helps you breathe. Come on, Josh, we'd better tend to business, here." She walked over and put up the toilet seat.

"It's *wood*, Shebby."

"Oak. Yes, it is." She started to help him pull down his sweats and underpants.

"I'll do it." He shoved her gently aside. "Boone showed me how to get my wee-wee out. Look. I don't gots to take my pants off. They gots a hole. See?"

"I see. Good for you." She swallowed a lump in her throat. How much longer would Boone be available to coach Josh in the art of being a boy? Maybe the end had already come.

BOONE, Sebastian and Travis trooped into the house. Travis had insisted on taking all Josh's toys and Sebastian had

Shelby and Josh's suitcases, so Boone had been left to carry only his duffel. Since nothing had been said about the baby, Boone finally decided he'd have to ask. "Where's Elizabeth?"

"Still back with Luann, I guess," Sebastian said over his shoulder. He glanced at Matty who had just come in the living room with a tray of drinks. "Where do you want us to put everything?"

"Luann?" Boone set his duffel down, not sure where he'd be sleeping yet. "What'd you do, hire a nanny?" He'd veto that quick. He didn't want his baby taken care of by strangers.

"Luann's my mother," Travis said. "Cool toys we have here, Sebastian. We can have ourselves some fun with—"

"Your *mother?*" Boone interrupted. "You never said anything about a mother. Where's she been all this time?"

"In Utah." Travis answer was nonchalant. "I see drinks are being served. Let's unload this stuff and party. Matty? What goes where?"

Matty set down the tray on the coffee table. "I thought we'd put—"

"Wait a minute," Boone said. "Do you mean to tell me, Travis, that when you went to Utah every winter, and we thought you were off playing with ski bunnies for six months, you were going to stay with your *mother?*"

"That's it," Sebastian put in before Travis could answer. "Hotshot pulled the wool over our eyes. Every winter he'd go home and take care of his mommy, like the good boy he is."

"Hey, there *were* a few ski bunnies!" Travis protested as well as he could, considering his chin was anchoring the pile of toys in his arms. "You're ruining my rep, here!"

Gwen came into the room with a bowl of chips and another of salsa. "You're getting married tomorrow. You don't need your rep anymore."

"I was a legend in Utah," Travis muttered. "No single woman was safe. That's my story and I'm sticking to it."

Matty chuckled. "Getting bridegroom jitters, Travis?"

"Not me. Just want to make sure the record's straight. Now, much as I'd love to stand around discussing my love life, these toys are heavier than they look. Where do they go?"

"I thought we'd put Josh back in with Elizabeth and I made up the daybed in Sebastian's office for Shelby."

Shelby and Josh reappeared at that moment. Josh went immediately to the rag rug by the fireplace where both dogs had plopped down. He began murmuring happily to them and rubbing their heads.

Shelby, however, glanced in obvious dismay at the load Travis and Sebastian were bringing in. "Boy, that's sure a pile of stuff. I promise we're not moving in, although you'd certainly think so."

Boone took a closer look at Shelby. Something about her had changed. When they'd first arrived, she'd seemed so happy to be here, but at the moment she didn't seem happy at all. He tried to catch her eye, but she seemed to be avoiding his gaze.

"Kids need a lot of things," Matty said. "Don't worry about it."

"See?" Boone said. "I told you it wouldn't be a problem."

Still Shelby wouldn't look at him. "I feel as if I've invaded your home," she said to Matty.

"Welcome invasion, if you ask me," Travis said. "Lizzie's toys were getting boring." He started down the hall. "I'll tell Mom to get a move on. She's probably fussing over every little ribbon, trying to make Lizzie perfect for her new audience."

Shelby's head snapped around and she stared down the hall after Travis. "Did he say *mom?*"

"Yeah, he did," Sebastian said as he passed her carrying her suitcase and Josh's. "Luann's been in there for the past hour dolling Elizabeth up."

Shelby turned to gaze at Boone with a smile, and the haunted look was gone from her eyes. "Travis's mom."

"Yeah." Boone didn't know what had caused Shelby to relax again, but he was glad she had. "I guess she's moved here from Utah. I didn't know—"

"Oh, that's wonderful," Shelby said in a breathless rush. Her smile widened. "Absolutely wonderful."

"I guess so." He thought it was okay, and probably nice for Travis, but he couldn't figure out why Shelby was so excited about the prospect. Still, he was glad she looked normal again.

Matty glanced over at him. "Is the couch okay for now?"

"Sure." He had no problem giving up his usual bed in Sebastian's office to Shelby.

Shelby's happy smile faded. "Oh, dear. I'll bet you usually sleep on that daybed, don't you?"

He shrugged. "Doesn't matter."

"I don't want to take your bed."

Josh glanced up from petting the dogs. "Let's all sleep together!" he said. "Like last night! We can cuddle."

Shelby sent Boone a horrified look. He became aware that Matty and Gwen were studying him, and he could feel the heat climbing up from his collar.

"It wasn't the way it sounds," Shelby said quickly, filling the silence. "Boone was sleeping in the chair, but the heat went out, and Josh was getting cold, so Boone came in with us, for more body heat, and..." Her voice trailed off, and now *her* cheeks were pink, too.

Boone felt responsible for her being embarrassed. If he

hadn't groped her in bed this morning, she'd probably be able to tell the story without blushing. As it was, Matty and Gwen had apparently figured out something was going on, judging from their smug expressions. They probably had the same idea Sebastian and Travis did, that Boone was coupled up with Shelby. For everybody's sake, he needed to squash that notion.

"You know, maybe I'll sleep in the barn," he said.

"We don't have dormitory rules here," Matty said, her blue eyes sparkling. "You can sleep wherever you want, Boone."

"I wanna sleep in the barn!" Josh scrambled to his feet and ran over to Boone to gaze up at him. "Can I sleep in the barn with you and the horsies?"

"Actually, Josh," Matty said. "I really was hoping you'd be willing to sleep in Elizabeth's room. She's so little, and she gets lonesome in there. She needs a big strong boy to keep her company."

"She does?"

"Ready or not," Travis called as he came back down the hall. "He-rrre's Lizzie!"

Boone had been so absorbed in trying to help Shelby out of an embarrassing moment, he'd forgotten the baby was coming. He turned toward the hallway, his gut clenching.

A gray-haired, wiry woman dressed in jeans and a sweatshirt walked in holding...an angel. Boone stared, speechless with wonder at the vision in pink ruffles. She had little pink ribbons tied in her soft brown hair, and little pink booties on her feet. Her creamy skin and tiny pink mouth looked too perfect to be real.

She turned her head and looked right at Boone.

He gazed into those eyes, so like his father's blue-gray ones. She stared at him with such seriousness, such complete attention, almost as if she *knew* him. His doubts faded away. Elizabeth was his.

"Hey, Lizzie." Travis walked over toward the baby. "Show Boone what you can do. Come on, like I taught you."

The baby stuck out her little tongue and blew a juicy raspberry at him.

The males in the room, including Josh, all laughed.

"Atta girl!" Grinning, Travis scooped her out of his mother's arms. "Awesome."

"Honestly, Travis," Luann said. "Teaching that sweet little girl tricks like that. You ought to be ashamed of yourself. And it doesn't help that you boys laugh at her, either. You're setting a bad example." She glanced pointedly at Josh.

Travis seemed unfazed. "I figure Lizzie will need that trick someday. Mom, I'd like you to meet Boone Connor, the blacksmith for the Rocking D and some of the other ranches around the valley. And this pretty lady is Shelby McFarland, who rode up here with Boone. And the little guy is Josh. Folks, this slightly square but basically lovable woman is my mom, Luann Evans."

Boone tipped his hat to Luann. "Pleased to meet you, ma'am." He held Luann's gaze for as long as necessary to be polite, but quickly his attention returned to Travis holding that baby. The little girl reminded him of cotton candy, all pink and sweet-smelling. Sure, she was drooling a bit, but that only made her cuter. He wanted to hold her, but he was afraid he'd goof it up.

"I'm glad to meet you, too, Mrs. Evans." Shelby stood and shepherded Josh over toward Travis's mother. "Josh, can you shake the nice lady's hand?"

"Yep. But I wish I had a hat, like Boone. Then I could touch my hat 'stead of shaking hands."

Distracted as he was by watching Elizabeth, Boone took

note of the comment and promised himself he'd see about a hat for Josh in the next couple of days. If the boy was going to ride a horse, then he needed a hat. Maybe boots, too.

"Please call me Luann," Travis's mother said as she leaned down to shake Josh's hand.

"Are you a gramma?" Josh asked.

Josh's innocent question was met with silence, and Boone realized that was probably a touchy subject, considering the battle to claim this baby. As he tried to think how to smooth over the moment, everyone started talking at once. Travis insisted that his mother was indeed a gramma, while Sebastian said the jury was still out on that, although he appreciated all Luann had done. Gwen said at the very least Luann was an honorary gramma, and Matty added that Elizabeth needed all the grammas she could get, so why not?

"My gramma's in heaven," Josh said. The announcement splashed like a bucket of water over the heated discussion, and everybody stopped arguing immediately as they all turned to gaze sympathetically at the little boy.

Everyone except Boone. He looked at Shelby, to see how the comment was affecting her. She met his gaze, and his heart ached as he watched the emotions raging in her blue eyes. Then she swallowed, and sent him a shaky smile. She wanted to let him know she was okay. It was all he could do to keep from crossing the room and taking her in his arms.

Of all the others in the room, Luann recovered herself first. She crouched down in front of Josh, and her voice was gentle. "In that case, how about if you call me Gramma Luann?"

Boone decided then and there that Luann Evans was all right.

"'Kay," Josh said hesitantly. "But do I gots to wear a tie?"

"A tie?" Luann glanced questioningly at Shelby.

"He means a necktie," Shelby cleared her throat.

"My...mother liked him to dress up when he went any-where with them."

Boone's heart squeezed. Poor little shaver, expected to dress up at this young age, just as Shelby had been forced to do when she was a kid. He didn't like to think ill of the dead, but he had a hard time thinking well of Shelby's parents, from what he'd heard so far.

"No, Josh," Luann said. "You don't have to wear a tie. Are you hungry?"

"Yep. Kinda hungry. They gots chips over there."

"I see those, but I was thinking of something like peanut-butter toast."

"I *love* that. Bob, he loves it, too."

Luann studied Josh for a moment and then she smiled. "I'll bet Bob is your special friend."

Boone exchanged another quick glance with Shelby, and this time her smile was brighter. Boone gave her a discreet thumbs-up sign. He was damned impressed that Luann had tuned into the Bob thing so fast. He could see the advan-tages of having an experienced mother around. Maybe that's why Shelby had been so excited when she'd found out Travis's mother was here.

Josh's eyes lit up. "Yep, he is my special friend! How'd you know?"

"Well, because Travis had a special friend when he was about your age. He always dressed in orange and pink, and his name was—"

"*Mom.*"

Boone couldn't believe that Travis, the ever-cool stud-man, was blushing. Sebastian was doing his level best to keep from laughing, and Gwen and Matty seemed to sud-denly find the pattern in the rag rug very interesting.

"Well, never mind," Luann said, glancing at her son with a grin. "I'll tell you all about it in the kitchen. Let's go make some peanut-butter toast for you and Bob." She stood and held out her hand.

Josh looked from Luann's outstretched hand to the baby girl in Travis's arms. "Can that baby come, too?"

No, Boone thought. *Not until I've had a chance to—*

"I think that's an excellent idea," Luann said. "Then you two can get acquainted."

"Can she play trucks?" Josh asked, clearly fascinated by the baby.

"Not yet," Luann said. "But she loves peekaboo."

"I can play that!" Josh's eyes shone with eagerness.

"It's settled, then." Luann retrieved Elizabeth from Travis, and with the baby propped on her hip and Josh holding her other hand, she walked back to the kitchen.

"Maybe she likes pirate ships," Josh chattered as he skipped along. "I gots a pirate ship, too. And little people. Me and Bob, we play pirates a lot."

Both dogs lifted their heads, lumbered to their feet and followed the three into the kitchen.

"Bless your mother, Travis," Shelby said after they'd left.

"Oh, she's a peach, that mother of mine." He crossed his eyes.

Gwen sidled over to him, a wicked gleam in her eyes. "So, Travis, what was your special friend's name, the one who dressed so tastefully in orange and pink?"

"Never mind."

"Yeah, Travis," Sebastian said. "You're just full of surprises these days. But did your mom get mixed up? If you went to all the trouble of making up a friend, it would have to be a girl, wouldn't it?"

Travis hooked his thumbs in his belt loops. "You know what? I have no idea what my mother was talking about. You'll have to forgive her. She's getting senile."

"Don't give me that. Your mother's sharp as a tack," Sebastian said.

Matty started lifting drinks from the tray on the coffee table. "I for one think it's charming that you had a little imaginary friend dressed in orange and pink, Travis. Now who wants something? Shelby, here's your wine, and another glass for Gwen. I have a draft for each of the guys, and—"

"Thanks," Boone said, "but I'm not having any beer."

"Oh, sure," Travis said. "An Irishman who won't bend an elbow at the bar. Since when?"

"Since the day I found out about Elizabeth."

Sebastian picked up his mug of beer and glanced at Boone, his gray eyes lit with challenge. "And that would be because..?"

Boone lowered his voice. "Don't get me wrong. Now that Elizabeth's here, I'm glad she was born and everything. But it shouldn't have happened in the first place. If I hadn't been drinking, it wouldn't have."

"Oh, I think it would have," Travis said easily. "Because once I'm bound on a course, you wouldn't have talked me out of it, even if you had been sober."

"You're making a powerful assumption, Travis," Sebastian said with an edge to his voice. "Let's not forget where Jessica decided to leave Elizabeth in the first place."

"You were closest!" Travis said. "Doesn't mean a thing!"

Matty sighed. "I guess we'd better hide the table knives, Gwen. It's starting again."

"Exactly what we figured would happen when Boone arrived," Gwen said. "The arguments will triple."

"There's nothing to argue about," Travis insisted stubbornly. "Lizzie's my kid."

"She's mine," Sebastian said. "She has the Daniels nose."

"She has my father's eyes!" Boone said.

Shelby set down her wineglass on the coffee table. "Since

I'm the new kid on the block, somebody needs to fill me in before I get terminally confused."

Everyone seemed ready to offer an explanation to Shelby except Boone, who decided he'd be too embarrassed to explain it all, especially considering he'd been the one who'd actually committed the shameful deed. The others might like to think they did, but Boone knew in his heart who had.

Finally Matty called for order and sat next to Shelby on the sofa. "I'll tell it." She looked over at Shelby. "Bear with me. This gets confusing. Two years ago this April, these three guys plus another friend, Nat Grady, were in an avalanche in Aspen."

Boone was amazed by the look of terror on Shelby's face as she glanced up at him. The idea that he'd been in danger seemed to hit her hard. He kind of liked that.

"Jessica Franklin was working at the ski lodge then, and she'd agreed to go out skiing with the guys, because she realized they were totally inept."

"Hey!" Sebastian said. "We weren't so bad."

Matty didn't even acknowledge the protest with a glance. "They stunk," she said. "Jessica's probably the only reason they survived. Nat was completely buried in the avalanche, but Jessica knew what to do. She figured out where he was and directed the operation while the guys dug him out."

"Wow," Shelby said.

"It was pretty dramatic, all right," Matty said. "Anyway, the next year the guys and Jessica decided to have an avalanche reunion party, only at the last minute Nat couldn't make it, so it was just the three guys and Jessica."

"Yeah," Boone asked. "Has anybody heard anything from Nat since he went over to that place in the Middle East—what was the name of it?"

"I can't ever remember," Sebastian said. "I think they changed the name a couple of times, at least, after they overthrew the dictator. But no, he's been totally out of touch. Matty thought she saw him on the news the other night when they had footage of some Americans who were over there working with the refugees, specifically the kids."

"I know he's doing a good thing over there," Boone said, "but I wish he'd come back home."

"Yeah, me, too," Travis said. "He borrowed my best sheepskin vest to wear over there. If I'd have known he'd be gone this long, I would have told him to buy his own damn vest."

Gwen rolled her eyes. "I'm so sure it's the vest you're worried about."

"Well, I'd rather not get it back with bullet holes in it," Travis said.

"I wish he'd come back so he could help Matty and me do the paperwork for combining our two spreads," Sebastian said. "And we've been talking about selling a few acres of hers. I wouldn't trust that to any broker but Nat."

Boone nodded. "Better wait'll he comes back."

"Yeah, you'd better wait," Travis agreed.

"I hope I don't have to wait that long to hear the end of the story," Shelby said.

"The rest goes fast," Matty said. "The guys all got ploughed, and Jessica didn't. She seems to have a guardian-angel thing going. She drove them all back to their rented cabin and tucked them in. Nine months later, Elizabeth was born, and two months after that, Jessica left her on Sebastian's front porch with a note asking him to be her godfather, because she was in desperate trouble and couldn't take care of her for a while. He, of course, assumed he'd done the deed while he was drunk. The thing is, she also sent a note like that to Travis and Boone, and they both assume the same thing."

Boone couldn't keep quiet any longer. "The notes to Travis and Sebastian were just a smoke screen. I'm the guy."

Travis turned to him. "Says who?"

"Yeah." Sebastian set his beer mug on the mantel. "How do you figure, Boone?"

Heat warmed his cheeks, and he couldn't look at Shelby. He'd rather not admit this in front of her, but it needed to be said. "Because I'm the strongest, the only one she couldn't have gotten away from, even if I was drunk."

"Oh, yeah?" Travis set his beer mug on a lamp table. "Maybe she didn't *want* to get away from me. Maybe—"

"Maybe we should have some dinner." Matty stood. "Life always looks less complicated on a full stomach."

Shelby stood and gazed around at the three cowboys. "So you three are *fighting* about who gets to claim Elizabeth?"

"You've got it," Matty said.

"Most men would be ducking out the back door in a case like this," Shelby said.

Gwen glanced at her. "If you stick around awhile, you'll soon discover that these aren't most men."

"I guess not," Shelby said. She looked into Boone's eyes. "No, I guess not."

He gazed back at her. He'd expected her to be disgusted with him for forcing a woman to have sex. Instead admiration shone from her blue eyes. Maybe she didn't really believe that he was the one.

"I am Elizabeth's father," he said quietly, looking into her eyes so she'd know he was telling the truth. He didn't want her spinning any daydreams about him.

"Like hell you are," Sebastian grumbled.

"Time to eat!" Matty said brightly, and led the way into the dining room.

10

SHELBY WAS SEATED next to Boone, which she suspected Matty had done on purpose. With all the people at the table, it was close quarters, and her knee was in constant contact with Boone's thigh. They bumped elbows more times than she could count, and her shoulder brushed his if she moved even slightly in his direction. Once, as he reached for the dish she was passing him, his forearm grazed her breast. She felt it clear to her toes, and she knew from the flush on his cheeks that he was completely aware of the intimate contact.

As if that weren't enough to start her engine running, everyone at the table treated them as a couple. Their names were linked often in the course of the conversation, and everyone kept giving them knowing looks. Surely they wouldn't do that if they knew Boone was in love with Jessica, Shelby thought. Maybe, just maybe, Jessica and the baby weren't such an insurmountable obstacle after all.

Holding Elizabeth during the meal was a privilege, apparently, and everyone vied for the chance to do it except Boone, Shelby noticed. He was the only one who held back, although she could plainly see that he wanted to. She'd decided the next time she had Elizabeth, she'd simply hand the baby over to Boone.

Near the end of the meal she was about ready to ask Luann for a turn with the baby when Sebastian raised his glass. "I have a more schmaltzy speech planned for tomorrow, but that doesn't mean we can't toast the happy couple tonight. Long life and happiness, Travis and Gwen."

"Same here," Boone said, raising his water glass. His arm brushed Shelby's in the process, but it had happened so many times they'd both stopped apologizing for bumping each other.

He'd still refused to have a drop of liquor. Later the men were planning a modified bachelor party at the Buckskin, a saloon in Huerfano, and Boone had vowed he'd stick to soft drinks there, too.

Shelby raised her wineglass. "I'm thrilled to be here, tickled pink for you, and I have no idea what I'll wear to the wedding."

Matty laughed. "I'll loan you something." She lifted her water glass. "Here's to Travis and Gwen, the surprise match of the year."

"And a darn good one." Luann touched her wineglass to Matty's. "Right, Elizabeth?"

From her perch on Luann's lap, the baby chortled happily.

Josh, who was sitting on two telephone books so he'd be the right height for the table, held up his milk glass in imitation of the grown-ups. "Yippee!" he said.

"I think that sums it up," Sebastian said with a smile. "Yippee, you two."

Everyone had clinked glasses and taken sips by the time Travis looked over at Matty. "What's with the water, Matilda? I just now noticed you haven't had any wine all night. Don't tell me Boone's new program is catching on?"

"Oh, I felt like having water tonight," Matty said a little too casually.

"But this is a celebration!" Travis said. "You've always been a celebrating kind of gal, Matty."

Matty exchanged a quick glance with Sebastian. Even

Shelby, who hadn't been around long, could tell the two had a secret.

Gwen must have caught the look, because she squealed and leaped up to run around the table. "You're pregnant!" she cried, hugging Matty fiercely.

"I didn't want to steal your thunder." Matty looked teary-eyed and happy. "This is supposed to be your time in the spotlight."

"Nonsense." Gwen dabbed at her eyes. "Oh, Matty, this is wonderful."

Shelby felt a stab of envy. She'd loved being an aunt and stand-in mom for Josh. Having a baby of her own would be heaven, especially with the right sort of man.... She glanced sideways at Boone, who was looking a little wistful himself. Right sort of man, wrong sort of circumstances. Ah, but how his solid presence next to her made her ache with longing.

"Preggers?" Travis drew everyone's attention as he scowled at Sebastian. "You knew this outstanding fact and you didn't tell Boone and me, your best friends in the whole world?"

"Second best." Sebastian smiled at his wife. "You've been downgraded. Matty's my best friend now."

Travis clutched his breast. "I'm cut to the quick. How about you, Boone?"

"We've been betrayed." Boone barely contained a grin. "I think this calls for strong measures."

Watching him, Shelby felt warmth flood through her. Boone was sexier than any man had a right to be. Circumstances or no circumstances, she'd love to know what a kiss from Boone would feel like. She wondered what he'd do if she took the initiative, sometime when they were alone. In this house, that might be never.

"Strong measures, indeed," Travis agreed. He pushed back his chair.

"Hold it, guys," Sebastian said. "Matty made me promise not to tell anybody. It's all her fault."

"Now he's hiding behind a woman's skirts," Boone said. He pushed back his chair and stood, flexing his hands. "Can't get much more cowardly than that, right, Travis?"

"Not much, Boone."

Shelby couldn't help but look at those strong fingers and remember how they'd felt cradling her breast.

"Time to teach Sebastian a little lesson," Boone said.

Josh's eyes grew round. "What're you gonna do?" His voice trembled.

Boone immediately turned and gave the little boy a smile of reassurance. "Nothing bad, Josh. Don't be afraid. We'll just roll him in a snowbank. I noticed there were still a couple down by the barn. It's a tradition around here when a guy gets his wife pregnant."

"A tradition that's about two minutes old." Sebastian's chair scraped on the wooden floor as he stood and faced his friends with a cocky grin. "*If* you can get it off the ground, which I doubt."

"If you break any dishes getting him outside," Matty warned, "I'll have all of your hides."

"You notice she didn't beg for us to spare you," Travis said, laughing. "So much for your best friend, Sebastian, old buddy. Loyalty ain't what it used to be."

"You know I never allowed roughhousing indoors, Travis Edward!" Luann said.

"Then I guess we'll have to take him outside," Travis said. "Ready, Boone?"

"Ready when you are, studman."

"Then let's get the new poppa."

Shelby was amazed that in the ensuing struggle only one glass was overturned and some silverware clattered to the floor. Travis and Boone managed to carry Sebastian out the back door without breaking a single dish.

The physical struggle excited Shelby more than she cared to admit, though. She watched Boone wrestle with Sebastian and wanted that sort of contact for herself. Boy, did she want it.

Matty was on her feet the minute they slammed out the back door. "We can watch from the kitchen window."

Shelby helped Josh out of his chair. "Do they do this kind of thing often?" she asked as she went with Matty, Gwen and Luann into the kitchen.

Matty chuckled. "To be honest? Yes. At the slightest excuse."

"This is more than a slight excuse." Gwen hugged Matty again. "How could you even think of keeping this a secret until after the wedding?"

"I had my time to be fussed over," Matty said. "I want this to be yours."

"Don't worry. This news will only add to the celebration."

Whoops and shouts of laughter, sprinkled with a few rich curse words floated back up to the house from the area down by the barn where the men wrestled in a small patch of snow lit by a dusk-to-dawn light.

Matty, Gwen, Luann and Shelby crowded around the window over the kitchen sink, each of them trying to get a glimpse of what was going on. Shelby lifted Josh up so he could see, and Luann held Elizabeth.

"Look at those crazy idiots," Gwen said with a chuckle. "You'd think they were all about five years old."

"I'm three years old," Josh announced proudly. "I builded a snowman. He's comin' alive. Can I build another one, Shebby? They gots some snow here."

"Maybe tomorrow," Shelby said. Then she remembered

the wedding. "If there's time. When's the ceremony, Gwen?"

"Not until seven," Gwen said. "That'll give my brother time to fly in from Boston, and then, too, we wanted to have candlelight."

"I'll bet it'll be beautiful."

"It will," Matty said, "as long as all the guys don't end up with black eyes and broken noses. I wonder if we should break up the happy party down there before that happens. When they horse around like this, they sometimes forget and actually do damage to each other by mistake."

"Horsies!" Josh said, latching onto Matty's statement. "I wanna see the horsies sleepin'!"

"That's right," Shelby said. "Boone did promise to take Josh down to the barn before bedtime so he could at least look at the horses."

"I wanna go," Josh said. "And Bob, he does, too."

"We're not going to disappoint Josh or Bob," Luann said. "Gwen, if you'll take Elizabeth, I'll go with Josh down to the barn and on the way I'll tell those big lugs to knock it off before they end up looking like prizefighters in the wedding pictures tomorrow."

"I'd like to go, too," Shelby said eagerly before she stopped to think. Then she glanced at the pots and pans on the stove and remembered there were a ton of dishes to do. "On second thought, never mind. I can see the horses tomorrow."

"Spoken like a typical woman," Matty said with a chuckle. "Go on down to the barn, Shelby. Gwen and I can handle this mess in no time flat."

Shelby shook her head. "Nope. That's not fair. A bride-to-be shouldn't be ruining her nails with dishes, and then there's the baby to worry about, too. Let me either take care of her or do some dishes. I want to repay a little of your generosity in having me stay with you."

Gwen laughed. "You want to do something? You can help us make the table favors for the reception after the guys head for the Buckskin. That should be tedious enough to drive us all crazy. Now get going, all three—excuse me, I mean all *four* of you, before Travis busts his nose and has to breathe through his mouth while he's saying his vows."

Shelby tried to stick to her guns, but Matty and Gwen were formidable when they joined forces. Moments later Shelby, Josh and Luann had bundled up against the cold and were headed down toward the barn. Shelby held one of Josh's hands and Luann held the other while Josh chattered away. Luann had agreed to hold Bob's hand, and she promised Josh that Bob was keeping up just fine.

Ahead of them the three men rolled on the cold ground in a tangle of arms and legs, their laughter punctuated with colorful swearing as their breath clouded the cold air.

"You boys watch your language, now," Luann called out. "I don't want this child picking up any of those words."

"What child?" Boone asked, glancing up. Then he grunted as Sebastian used the moment to ram an elbow into his ribs.

"You three stop this nonsense immediately," Luann said, her voice ringing with authority. "You should all know better. Look at you. Half-frozen and your clothes a sight."

The men all stopped wrestling and looked shamefacedly at Luann. Shelby had to press her lips together to keep from laughing. They'd all been acting like five-year-olds, and now they even wore the expression of five-year-olds caught being naughty. Each of them would make about two of Luann, but she was obviously the one in charge at the moment.

"I guess you got a point, Mom." Travis stood slowly and

began brushing himself off as he surveyed his two partners in crime. "Looks like we ripped your sleeve, there, Sebastian."

"Yep." Sebastian sat up and glanced at it. "Matty'll have a fit."

Boone got up and held out a hand to help Sebastian to his feet. "Blame it on me, buddy. She'll probably go easier on me than she would on you." He glanced sheepishly at Josh. "How're you doin', Josh?"

"Shebby says I'm not s'posed to fight."

"And she's absolutely right," Boone said as he tucked his damp shirttail into his mud-smeared jeans. "We weren't really fighting. Just funnin'."

Shelby took in the heaving chest, the tousled hair, the mangled clothes, and it was all she could do not to sigh with longing. He was so damned earthy, so completely physical. She could eat him up with a spoon.

"But you ripped his *shirt*." Josh mimicked Luann's indignation perfectly. "And you gots mud all over."

"Yeah, and I'll probably need to buy him a new shirt and help Matty with the laundry," Boone said, looking guilty. "See, that's what I get."

"Yep," Josh said as if satisfied that Boone understood his transgressions. "That's what you get. We're gonna see the horsies sleepin'."

Boone looked even more guilty. "Oh, yeah. I said I'd take you, didn't I?"

"You're welcome to come along," Luann said crisply. "If you can behave yourself."

"Yeah, come along!" Josh let go of Shelby and Luann and ran over to gaze up at Boone. "Please?"

"Uh, okay." He glanced warily at Luann. "If you're sure."

"I'm sure," Luann said, her voice softening a little.

"*Okay*." Josh held out his hand. "Let's go."

"Wait a sec. I need to clean off my hand." Boone searched for a place on his jeans that wasn't covered with mud and finally found one large enough to wipe his hand on. "My hand's going to be cold, now," he warned as he leaned down to take Josh's.

"Then Bob and me, we'll warm you up! Like last night."

Shelby glanced at Luann with an apologetic smile. "I think we've been replaced," she said in a low voice.

Josh looked over his shoulder. "Come on, Gramma Luann. Come on, Shebby. Let's go see the horsies!"

"Not replaced," Luann said. "Included. That boy needs Boone like a plant needs sunlight."

"I know. I'm just worried—"

"My advice is to let him soak it up while he can," Luann said. "Now let's go see the horses."

Boone hadn't figured on Shelby and Josh coming down to the barn and catching him making a fool of himself wrestling with Sebastian. Had he known that would happen, he probably would have thought twice. He could see how Josh looked up to him, and he took that responsibility seriously.

He also didn't relish looking like a fool in front of Shelby. But she was part of the reason he'd gone along with Travis's idea to roll Sebastian in the snowbank. Sitting next to her at dinner and rubbing up against her every five seconds had worked him into quite a state. Wrestling with the guys was a good way to work off some steam, before he lost control and did something stupid with Shelby.

"Hey, Boone!" Travis called after them. "All three of us may be sleeping in the barn tonight, so throw some clean hay into a stall while you're at it, buddy."

"Uh-huh," Boone called back. "I suppose you'd like a mint on your pillow, too, hotshot?"

Travis laughed as he started up to the house beside Sebastian, who was limping slightly. "Fresh flowers would be a nice touch," he bellowed over his shoulder.

"You gots flowers?" Josh asked as Boone let go of his hand to slide the bolt open on the barn door. "Shebby loves flowers."

"Then maybe we should get her some pretty soon," Boone said. He wondered when Shelby had last had somebody bring her flowers. And she deserved them, for all she'd been through. He mentally added another item to his shopping list for the time when he took Josh into town for a hat and boots. Probably the day after the wedding.

Getting Shelby flowers might not be the wisest thing to do, because he wasn't in a position to ask her out or anything, but still, he'd love seeing the look on her face when he gave them to her. And she really did deserve some.

Boone led the way into the warmth and darkness of the barn and felt a thrill of sexual awareness, knowing Shelby was close behind him. City kids made out in the back seats of cars, but country kids, which Boone had been, usually learned about sex in the privacy of a barn. He'd lost his virginity to Darlene in a soft bed of hay.

"Smells good in here," Josh whispered, his voice trembling with excitement.

"Yep. I think so, too." Boone turned on a small battery-operated light Sebastian had mounted on the wall inside the door. It would allow them to see, just barely, without exciting the horses and making them think it was feeding time.

Boone glanced back at Luann and Shelby. "Can you two see okay?"

"I'm fine," Shelby said.

"Me, too," Luann added. "Come here, Josh. Let me hold you up so you can look over the stall doors."

"Boone can hold me," Josh said.

Boone eased the door closed to keep the barn warm. "I

would, Josh, but I'm kinda dirty. Shelby probably wouldn't want you to get any mud on you."

"Oh, I'll bet Shelby won't mind too much," Luann said.

"No, of course not," Shelby said.

So Boone picked Josh up, trying to keep him away from the worst of the mud while they started down the row of stalls. Boone whispered the names of the horses as they came to each stall, and all four of them stood and gazed into the shadowy depths at the horse lying or standing quietly inside. Luck was with them, and Samson roused himself enough to come to the stall door.

Josh held his breath and leaned down to carefully stroke Samson's nose. "See you tomorrow, Samson," he murmured. "Now, go sleepy-bye."

Josh didn't want to leave Samson's stall, but Boone knew it must be getting close to Josh's bedtime, so he coaxed him away and continued the tour. Gradually Josh relaxed in his arms, and eventually began to yawn, even though he was obviously fighting sleep so he could stay in the barn.

His head drooped closer and closer to Boone's shoulder, until at last it rested there. Boone discovered he absolutely loved the feeling of the little guy falling asleep in his arms.

"Somebody's out like a light," Luann said in a low tone. "Why don't you let Shelby or me carry him up to the house, Boone?"

"I'll do it," Boone said.

"That won't work very well," Luann said. "You're going to have to strip down before you go in that house."

"Good point." He wondered how Sebastian and Travis had handled that problem. Stripping down outside in this weather would be cold as hell. And Matty had been cleaning for days getting ready for the wedding, so she wouldn't take kindly to people traipsing through her house with mud on their clothes.

"Tell you what," Luann said. "You stay here where it's warm. Shelby and I will take Josh up to the house, and one of us will bring you some clean clothes. I'm sure you've got a sink or a hose or something in this barn, so you can wash up a little. How's that?"

"Okay." It sounded much better than what Sebastian and Travis must have been put through, so he decided to grab the opportunity.

"Here," Shelby said, moving close to Boone. "Let me take Josh."

Gradually Boone transferred Josh to Shelby, which involved more touching, plus he got a good whiff of her cologne. He must not have blown off as much steam during the wrestling match as he'd hoped, because he was right back in a state of agitation. Worse yet, the dim light in the barn reminded him of the night before, when he'd been in bed with Shelby and wrapped himself around her in his sleep. The potent image grabbed him in a very specific area and started working on him.

"Got him," Shelby whispered. "Thanks, Boone."

"No problem," he lied, his voice husky. Major problem. He wanted her so much he could hardly breathe. He wondered if Travis's wedding tomorrow was putting ideas in his head, or maybe even Matty's announcement tonight had started him thinking about babies and how much fun it would be to make one. Whatever it was, Shelby had become an incredibly strong temptation, one he had to resist. Somehow.

"Okay," Luann said as she started toward the door of the barn. "One of us will be back down in a jiffy with fresh clothes."

Boone stared after them. He knew who would be the safest person to bring him some clothes. It was not the person he wanted to bring them.

11

BOONE CONVINCED himself that Luann would be the logical choice to bring him his clothes. Shelby would be busy tucking Josh into bed. So it seemed safe to take off his mud-encrusted shirt and use the big utility sink Sebastian had installed near the front door of the barn to wash off at least part of the grit.

The water was cold, but not too bad. After cleaning his hands, arms and neck, he stuck his head under the faucet to rinse the mud out of his hair. Then he found an old but clean towel on a nearby shelf and rubbed it over his head. As he thought about that wrestling match, he began to grin.

Carrying Sebastian outside and throwing him in the snowbank might not have been the most mature thing to do, but it had been fun. After growing up with two sisters he'd always treated with great care, it was a relief to let go and have some fun with a couple of friends who gave as good as they got.

Although he might be bigger and a little stronger than Sebastian and Travis, they both had some moves that made them worthy wrestling opponents. Yeah, rolling around in the snow and working off his excess energy had felt great, especially after being cooped up in the truck for so many hours with a woman he wasn't supposed to want, a woman he couldn't stop craving.

The barn door creaked open, and he turned, expecting Luann.

Instead, Shelby stood in the pale light from the battery lamp with a bundle of his clothes in her arms. She nudged the door closed with her foot. "I...I had to guess what you might want me to bring," she said.

"Anything." He cleared his throat. "Anything's fine." His heart began to race. So she had decided to bring his clothes. He wondered if she knew how dangerous a move she'd just made. They'd never been really, truly alone until this moment. Surely she'd thought of that before she'd set out for the barn. Or maybe she had no idea he was on fire for her.

She'd caught him half-naked this morning, too. He'd been embarrassed then, but now...now he was too far gone for embarrassment. Long agonizing hours of wanting her had worn him down, and he was crazy to hold her warm body close.

With his shirt gone they were one step closer to what he'd been thinking about all day. One more tempting step. And that was why, if he had thought she'd bring his clothes instead of Luann, he would have left his shirt on.

She walked toward him and held out the clothes. "I, um, brought underwear, too." Even the weak light from the lamp picked up the bloom in her cheeks. "I wasn't sure if the snow got down in...well, I wanted you to have that option of changing your..."

Her explanation ran out of steam as she gazed at him, her lips parted, her breathing unsteady. Her ski jacket was open in front, as if she'd unzipped it in the house while she gathered his clothes and then hurried down here without bothering to zip it up again.

Or maybe she'd left it open on purpose. Maybe there wasn't a single innocent thing about this trip to the barn. He swallowed. "Thanks." He took the clothes and his hand brushed hers. His heart nearly stopped. Her skin was so warm. So soft. She would feel like that everywhere. Oh, God.

"I like your friends so much, Boone," she went on, chattering as if standing here in the semidarkness was no big deal. As if they weren't moments away from a major decision. "Here I've burst in on the wedding festivities and yet they're making me feel completely welcome, as if having me and Josh around is no trouble."

He forced himself to say something, anything. "I'm sure they're glad to have you." He could barely see straight from wanting to touch her again. But he knew damned well touching Shelby would be like the potato-chip ad. He wouldn't be able to stop with just one.

"They act as if they are glad. Luann asked if she could put Josh to bed because it had been so long since she'd tucked a little boy in and she missed it so. Isn't that sweet?"

"Yeah. Luann's great." He sounded hoarse, as if he had a cold coming on. But it was heat, not cold that was running through him right now. He was a fool to keep playing with fire, to stand here half-naked talking to Shelby, but he couldn't seem to walk away from the blaze. "And she caught onto the Bob thing real quick." He didn't want to talk about Luann. *Touch me, Shelby.*

"I know. And when she asked Josh to call her Gramma Luann, I could have kissed her."

He nearly groaned. Sure enough, now he couldn't stop looking at her mouth. She had a world-class mouth—full lips shaped like an archer's bow, framing perfect white teeth. Kissing her would be better than winning the lottery. "Guess I should change my clothes and get on up to the house." But for some reason, instead of stepping back from her, which would let her know she should leave, he moved a little closer.

"I'm not sure I brought the right things." She seemed to be edging closer to him, too.

He watched the movement of her lips as she spoke, and he lost track of what she was saying as he imagined fitting his mouth to hers and exploring all that perfection with his tongue. Then he would thrust deep, to let her know what was really on his mind, and she would mold herself against him. And this was a woman with the curves to do it right.

"Maybe you should check through them before I leave."

He had no idea what she was talking about. "Check through what?"

"Your clothes." Her gaze held his, and her voice was breathy and soft. "In case you want me to take something back and bring you something else."

His nostrils flared as he breathed in her scent, and his groin tightened. There was a soft sheen on her lips, as if she'd run her tongue over them before coming into the barn. "I'm not fussy...about clothes," he said. *Only about the women I kiss.*

"You're sure?" Her eyes darkened.

The lack of light had probably made her eyes do that, he told himself. "These will be fine," he said. But she might be aroused. If she was, he should ignore it. Like hell he would, when he was trembling with the need to hold her. He gazed into those eyes, searching for heat to match his own. There. Maybe. Yes...no...

She laid her hand on the pile of clothes he held in his arms. "Because if you want something else..."

She'd leaned in close enough that he felt her warm breath on his chest. His nipples tightened. He wanted something else all right, something he had no right to ask for. "Shelby—"

"Boone Connor, if you don't kiss me in the next two seconds I'm going to explode."

He dropped the clothes and swept her up in his arms with a groan of surrender. Contact. At last. "This is a mistake," he murmured. They were the last coherent·words he spoke as he found her mouth and lost his mind.

She was so light, no heavier than a child in his arms. Yet this was no child he was kissing. Her mouth was a woman's mouth, hot and eager. He'd meant to explore, maybe even to tease, but she parted those full lips and gave him an invitation he couldn't refuse. Her moan of delight when he pushed inside echoed throughout his body and settled heavily between his thighs.

He had to hunch down to keep his contact with her, and at first the wonder of her mouth and the openness of her response kept him so occupied he didn't mind. But a crick was developing in his neck, and besides, he wanted those full breasts right up against his chest.

He slipped an arm under her bottom to lift her so that her hungry mouth was level with his, and she wrapped her legs around his hips, exactly as he'd once imagined she would. *Ah, yes. There.* He felt the sensuous give of her breasts as he drew her in close.

But not close enough for her, it seemed. His pulse rate skyrocketed as she wrapped her legs even tighter around him, crushed her breasts against his bare chest and tilted her head back, inviting him deeper into her mouth. *Oh, Shelby.*

With a growl of need, he took what she offered and more, possessing her mouth with a frenzy that wasn't like him at all. He squeezed her so tight it was a wonder either of them could breathe. He'd thought of himself as gentle, deliberate, cautious. Not this time. Not with this woman.

She urged him on, and as his kisses became more intense she wrapped her legs tighter around him, putting sweet pressure right where he needed it. *Yes. Like that.* In a million years he wouldn't have imagined this much passion lurked within her. He didn't think women daydreamed about sex the way men did.

But Shelby acted as if she'd spent the past day building up as much frustration as he had. She began to rock against him, causing a maddening, wonderful friction against his chest...and lower, where his erection strained. As the tension ratcheted upward, she made little noises deep in her throat. Wild, needy sounds that shattered what little self-control he had left.

He backed her against the sink, propping her on the curved edge so his hands would be free. Free to reach inside the coat she'd left unzipped, free to pull her shirt from the waist of her jeans and reach up underneath to unfasten her bra. And all the while he drowned his conscience in the whirlpool of her kiss.

When he cupped her bare breasts her skin was hot as a furnace, and his caressing thumbs found her nipples already hard, thrusting eagerly against the pad of his thumb. His desire expanded. Now he wouldn't be satisfied until he took a warm, puckered nipple into his mouth, swirled the tip against his tongue, sucked and nibbled and licked until she became as wild with lust as he was.

Yet as he imagined tasting her breasts, he knew that wouldn't be enough. Maybe nothing would ever be enough, when it came to Shelby. He hadn't known he could ache like this, or that she would match him in her desperation.

Knowing she was as filled with repressed desire as he was made him want more, dare more. He gave up the heart-stopping pleasure of fondling her breasts so that he could tug off her coat. His blood surged when he realized she was helping him, wiggling out of the coat, pulling off her shirt.

Of course he shouldn't be doing this, but he couldn't stop and she wasn't about to stop him. This grinding need had been born when he'd woken this morning with her curled against his hot, hard penis. And it had never left. The need had been there underneath his thoughts about Fowler, his worry about Elizabeth, his joking with his friends. At last his need for her had burst free, and he was helpless before it.

He dragged his mouth from hers and supported her with an arm around her waist as she whipped the shirt off over her head, flinging it to the floor. Her bra followed.

Eyes hot, she held his gaze. Her mouth was swollen from his kisses, her skin pink from the scrape of his beard. As her breath came in quick little gasps, she braced a hand on each side of the sink...and arched her back.

"Oh, Lord." His heart beat so fast he thought he might need an ambulance soon. But he'd die a happy man, having seen such glory.

He'd been in a rush to rip away her clothes, but now her beauty, evident even in the dim light, awed him. He hesitated, afraid to touch her creamy breasts for fear of marring them. Her small frame made them even more spectacular, more lush and exotic. His breath caught as he stared in admiration.

"My heart is pounding like a rabbit's," she murmured. "Touch me there, Boone. I want you to feel my heart going like sixties."

He slowly laid a hand over her heart and his fingers curved naturally, cradling her fullness. Her heartbeat tapped against his palm, a secret code spelling out her desire. A miracle, that a beautiful creature like this wanted him so much. He flexed his fingers, kneading gently. Her nipple quivered, lifted, tempting him. A sweet raspberry of a nipple centered on the areola, ripe and ready to be plucked. His mouth grew moist.

Yet still he hesitated, gazing at his big, work-scarred hand cupping the satisfying weight of her breast. He thought of how his calloused fingers and his beard might scrape her tender skin. "My hands are so rough," he whispered. "And my beard, too. I'll give you a rash. I'll—"

"I want your rough hands," she said breathlessly. "I want your hungry mouth and your rough beard. I've spent the whole blessed day wishing you'd touch me like this."

He looked into her eyes. "I've been going insane."

"Oh, so have I," she whispered. "So have I. Take what you need. Give me what I need. Please."

And at last, he did. Gently at first. Carefully. Until passion built to a flood within him, washing away restraint. Then he feasted like a wild man, mindless to everything but pleasure, heedless of all else but her soft moans and choked words of encouragement.

And now he wanted more. Another time, another place he might have held back, chained by his own reluctance to trespass. But his life was spinning out of control, opportunities slipping away. Shelby was here, offering him these few stolen moments, this chance at forbidden pleasure. Her ripe body roused a demon within him, one that had no limits and would not be denied.

He'd made no conscious decision to unfasten her jeans, and he barely remembered working them and her panties over her hips, lifting her up like a rag doll in the process. It was merely a necessary step toward his goal.

And now he had what he wanted, as he crouched in front of her, his hands splayed across her bare bottom. All he knew was that she didn't stop him. She wasn't going to stop him. His blood ran hot in his veins.

Slowly, deliberately, he tasted. She gasped and quivered in his arms. Breathing in the primitive scent of aroused woman, he savored the rich nectar of her response on his tongue, and his mind filled with a red haze of passion. A low, urgent groan rose from her throat. He took his prize.

Ah, she was sweet. And so willing, so ready for whatever

he wanted. And he wanted. He trembled with wanting. He battled images of rising to his feet, ripping open his jeans and taking her completely. She was so open, so wet.

As he pushed her higher, the pressure to be deep inside her became almost beyond bearing. But he would bear it. She had endured so much. He would give her this. She was nearly there. Triumph welled within him. Yes, he would give her this.

As she climaxed, she bucked and quaked in his grip. Her muted cries of release thrilled him more than shouts of ecstasy, and he was overcome with a fierce possessiveness. Despite the painful ache in his groin, her satisfaction eased the sharp edge of his desire and made way for tenderness.

He kissed her moist curls. Then he guided her to his lap, trailing kisses over her belly, her ribs, her breasts, her throat. At last they were once more face-to-face.

Resting her hands on his shoulders, she gazed at him, her eyes filled with wonder.

He cupped her face in one hand and brushed his thumb over her cheek. The expression on her face made the torture in his groin well worth it. He'd never been so bold with a woman he'd known such a short time. They'd come a long way, considering that two days ago neither of them had known the other existed. And it was probable this was as far as they'd ever go.

He took a breath. "I'm afraid I got...carried away. Something let loose in me, I guess. Like a dam breaking."

She nodded. "I know. I walked...down here to see..." She paused and took a breath, herself. "To see if I could get you to kiss me."

A smile tugged at his mouth. "You broke the dam."

"Sure did," she murmured. "Blew it to smithereens. That was some kiss."

And now he knew what else he had to say. Not the loving

promises and pledges that he longed to make. No, he had to protect her from those, which would only hurt her. He would give her warnings, delivered with a smile that he hoped would take the sting out. "That might be the only one I can ever give you," he said. "I thought I'd make it count."

"You certainly did." She bracketed his face in her hands, and she seemed to want to ignore the first part of his statement. "But it was a one-sided kiss, Boone."

"It's better that way." And it was, he knew. Letting her go after what they'd just shared wouldn't be easy, but once he'd known the joy of burying himself deep inside her, letting her go would be impossible.

"Better because you get to stay in control and I don't?"

"Maybe." He took a deep breath. "But I wouldn't say I've been totally in control. I really didn't mean to..."

"And I didn't mean to let you." She combed her fingers through his damp hair as her gaze searched his. "But I did," she murmured. "So where are we now, Boone?"

"Probably in a hell of a mess. Nothing's changed for me."

"Nothing?"

"Not really." He sighed at her look of disappointment. "I know that's not what you'd like to hear. But the truth is, I wanted you before. The only difference is that now I know what I'll be missing."

Her jaw firmed under his grip and her eyes gleamed in the dim light. "Not by a long shot. This is the tip of the iceberg, mister."

"I was afraid of that." The ache that he thought he had under control began building again. To distract himself, he looked around for the clothes she'd tossed on the floor. He reached over and picked up her bra. Holding that lacy confection did nothing to ease his discomfort. He shook it to get any bits of straw out and handed it to her.

"My cue to make tracks?" she asked.

"People will start to wonder where you are."

"They know where I am. I get the impression they approve." She slipped the bra on and arched her back to fasten it from behind.

"I'm sure they do. But I have to handle this situation my way." He shouldn't watch her fasten her bra, not if he wanted to keep his sanity. Glancing around, he located her shirt and picked that up, too. "The way I see it, the more we get involved with each other, the tougher it'll be when you go back to San Antonio and I have to stay here to deal with Elizabeth and Jessica."

She remained silent, not disagreeing, but not agreeing, either.

Shaking out her shirt, he gave it to her. "Don't pin your hopes on me, Shelby. I'm not your fantasy cowboy. I have two people depending on me. They have a prior claim, and I mean to honor that."

She put her arms in the sleeves and pulled the shirt over her head. Then she gazed at him. "Boone, could it be possible, just slightly possible, that Elizabeth is not your child?"

"She's mine," he said, surprised at how much the question irritated him. One look into the baby's eyes and he was ready to fight for the title of daddy. "But even if she's not, Jessica asked me to be her godfather for the time being. So either way, I have an obligation to Elizabeth. And to Jessica." Wrapping his arms around Shelby, he lifted her up as he rose to his feet. He made sure she'd regained her balance before he loosened his grip.

"I see." She'd fastened her jeans and reached for her coat before she spoke again. "You probably think I'm shameless, coming down here tonight. Especially when you've made it clear that you don't want to get involved with me."

He caught her chin and made her look at him. "I am involved with you. I can't help myself. Everything that happened just now, I wanted as much as you, maybe more. I think you're a beautiful, sexy woman. But the timing stinks."

She nodded and put on her coat.

Her resolute expression tore at his heart. She'd had to stuff her feelings about her parents and sister getting killed in order to be strong for Josh. Now he was asking her to stuff her feelings about him, too. "I wish I could be what you need," he said, knowing how lame that must sound to someone who'd fought the inner battles Shelby had.

She took a long, shaky breath and shoved her hands in her pockets. Then she gave him a bold once-over, tilting her head in a cocky, devil-may-care way. "You might not be Mister Right, but you make a fantastic Mister Right Now. I had a great time."

His heart broke. He didn't want to be the cause of her putting on a brave front, but he was. "Me, too," he said softly.

"Tip of the iceberg," she said, turning on her heel. "You might want to remember that."

"I probably will." Like for the rest of his life.

She paused, her back to him. "I don't know what this Jessica person is doing running all over the countryside, when a man like you is waiting right here, willing and ready to protect and take care of her. She must be ten kinds of a fool." Then, her head held high, she left the barn.

After she left, Boone paced the length of the barn a few times until his body cooled down. Gradually the full impact of his behavior settled on his conscience, and finally he sat on a bale of hay and dropped his head in his hands.

For reasons that escaped him, Shelby still had him on some sort of pedestal. She ought to have him run out of town on a rail.

All his life he'd thought of himself as a gentleman, a guy who treated women with every consideration. Darlene had even complained that he was too *much* of a gentleman, but he'd explained that was the way he was made. He had such respect for her and all women that he had to be polite, even when making love.

What a crock. Given the right circumstances, he could be an animal. He could get drunk and make a good friend pregnant without her consent. Then, as if that wasn't bad enough, he could meet a stranger and within twenty-four hours have her stripped and moaning in his arms.

And in spite of the fact that he knew that it was wrong, wrong, wrong, he wanted to do it all again. He couldn't imagine a sweeter fate than to be locked in a bedroom with Shelby for about two weeks.

But even so, he was prepared to abandon her, telling her she had to be sacrificed to his noble principles. Ha. He had no stinkin' principles, at least when it came to one short, well-endowed blonde.

He'd damn well better get some, though, and fast. Shelby didn't deserve to be treated like that. From now on, he wasn't laying a hand on her. He was never touching that silky skin again. That warm, creamy skin...that tender mouth...those plump, tasty breasts...

He groaned. Life used to be so simple.

12

IF ANYBODY NOTICED Shelby's rumpled condition when she came back from the barn, they were polite enough not to mention it. She managed to escape to the bathroom and repair the damage to her appearance while Matty, Gwen and Luann hauled out the supplies for making the party favors.

The damage to her heart would require a little more than a comb and some makeup, though. There was no doubt Boone wanted her physically. She'd gotten a whole lot more than she'd bargained for tonight. But no matter how wonderful he'd made her feel, his lust wasn't enough to satisfy her. She wanted everything Boone had to offer, and it seemed he was saving himself for Jessica.

Frustrated as she felt, she couldn't blame him for that. He thought he and Jessica were the parents of a child. If so, then he'd made love to her, and Boone wasn't the sort of man to take that lightly. At this very moment he might be trying to think himself into falling in love with Jessica, to justify what had happened. And while his thoughts were centered on another woman, he couldn't very well let Shelby into his heart. Unfortunately he'd already found his way into hers.

By the time Boone came into the house, Sebastian and Travis were ready to head for the bachelor party at the Buckskin and the four women had begun assembling the favors at the dining-room table. Travis and Sebastian both came over to kiss their sweethearts goodbye.

Travis gave his mother a peck on the cheek, too. He dislodged her red granny glasses in the process, and although she pretended to be impatient with his gusto, Shelby could tell she was thrilled with the attention.

Shelby was the only one of the four who went kiss-free, and she was painfully aware of Boone's slightest movement as he waited for the others to say their goodbyes. Her skin flushed when she thought of the fevered kisses they'd so recently shared. And if she wasn't careful, she'd get caught giving him soulful glances.

Determined not to look like Miss Lonelyhearts, she aimed a brilliant smile in his general direction. "Have a great time!" she said cheerfully.

"How can he have a great time if he's drinking root beer?" Travis walked over and hooked an arm around Boone's neck as if to put him in a hammerlock.

Boone braced himself, looking as immovable as a bronze statue.

After Travis realized he couldn't knock his friend off balance, he gave up the effort with a grin. "It's not bad enough that he can usually beat me at arm wrestling even when he's drunk. Now that he's turned into a damned teetotaler I'll never win again."

"Somebody has to drive," Boone said. "I'm sure as hell not letting you have the keys, bridegroom."

Even the sound of Boone's voice made Shelby's whole body tingle. She'd have to get control of herself.

"None of you has to drive," Gwen said. "I think the three of you should crash at Hawthorne House tonight. That's walking distance from the Buckskin."

"*Walking* distance?" Sebastian looked offended. "You must have us confused with yuppie city slickers. We're big he-man cowboy types. We drive our manly trucks or we ride our manly steeds. We don't *walk*."

"Oh." Gwen grinned. "Excuse me. Then maybe you'd

like me to pick you studly dudes up when I come back into town?"

"No need," Boone said. "I'll be fine to drive. And I'm supposed to bring Travis back here, right?"

"If you're sure you're all not going to stay at Hawthorne House," Gwen said.

Sebastian adjusted the tilt on his Stetson. "Nope. Thanks for the invite, but we're coming back here."

"Okay," Gwen said. "Then, yes, please bring Travis back with you. Luann and I can get more done in the morning if he's not around."

"Fine talk," Travis grumbled. "This is your new husband you're talking about."

"Exactly," Luann added. "And it's traditional for the bride and groom to be separated the night before the wedding."

"Got it," Boone said. "See you all later. Come on, you party animals. Let's go."

See you all later. Shelby had been included in the crowd. No special look, no special words for her alone. It was as if the moments in the barn had been a fantasy.

"You *used* to be a party animal," Travis complained. "I don't know how one little ol' long-neck will compromise your honor." He continued his lament as they went out the front door. "Or two little ol' long-necks. Or—" The door closed after them.

Shelby went back to wrapping favors, her heart aching. She believed that Boone wouldn't drink tonight, but she almost wished he would. Maybe alcohol would unlock some of the secrets of his heart.

"I hope they'll be okay," Gwen said as Boone's truck pulled away.

"They will." Matty tied her blond hair back in a scrunchie before she continued wrapping chocolate kisses. "Boone won't have anything to drink. He and Sebastian both have a stubborn streak a mile wide."

"I like Boone," Luann said. "He seems solid and trustworthy."

"He is," Shelby said. "And I'm very grateful that he decided to help me and Josh."

"He plays his cards pretty close to his chest, though," Matty said. "Far as I know, he's only been in love once, and that didn't turn out well."

Jessica? Shelby couldn't ignore the possibility. Maybe Boone was in love with Jessica, but she didn't return his love. That would make him feel especially guilty about the baby. And he hadn't seen Jessica in more than a year. He was probably frustrated, both sexually and emotionally. Of course he'd react the way he had in the barn tonight. Maybe he would have reacted that way with any woman.

The phone rang, and Matty went to answer it.

A lump of misery clogged Shelby's throat, but this was supposed to be a joyous time for the other women at the table. From years of self-discipline, Shelby was able to swallow the lump in her throat and begin asking Gwen and Luann questions about the decorations for the wedding. Gwen would be a beautiful bride. Shelby imagined how perfectly a white wedding gown would contrast with her dark hair and eyes and the golden tone of her skin.

The last wedding Shelby had attended had been her sister's lavish extravaganza. Patricia had been married with plenty of glamour, but not a tenth of the joy Shelby knew would surround Gwen and Travis's ceremony. Poor, doomed Patricia. At least if Shelby found herself feeling weepy tomorrow she wouldn't be the only one in tears. Happy tears and sad tears probably looked about the same on the outside.

In the midst of Gwen's description of how she and Luann

had decorated the bed-and-breakfast and the surrounding Victorian garden for the reception, Matty returned.

"It was Jessica on the phone." Matty sounded weary.

Anger and jealousy coursed through Shelby. "What did she want?"

"The same. To know that Elizabeth's okay. That's all she ever asks and then she gets off the phone immediately. I could hear traffic in the background. I'm sure she was using a pay phone somewhere." Matty sat down again and picked up a chocolate kiss.

"But where?" Luann asked.

"Who knows?" Matty sighed and threw the piece of candy back in the pile. "I'm getting damned sick of this, you know? I think we hired a dud of a detective. He's turned up practically nothing, except to tell us she's been traveling all over the place, which we knew, anyway. She's always one step ahead of him. Maybe Sebastian and I should fire him and try somebody else."

"It is getting ridiculous," Gwen agreed. "We need to know which one of these guys is the father so we can all get on with our lives."

Shelby would be in favor of that, too. "Have you ever asked her about that when she calls?"

"We've tried," Matty said. "That's the point in the conversation where she hangs up. She doesn't want us to know who Elizabeth's father is, apparently. Or she's not willing to say on the phone. I did tell her just now that Boone is here, to get her reaction."

Shelby tried to keep the anxiety out of her voice. "And?"

"She just said 'good.' Then when I tried to ask if Boone was the baby's father, she hung up, like she always does."

Shelby began wrapping kisses again. So Jessica was happy that Boone was here. Maybe that meant she would be coming back. Maybe she'd decided she loved him, after all.

She might have been waiting for him to arrive. "Boone really thinks he's Elizabeth's father," she said.

"Which makes him absolutely no different from the other two," Gwen said. "Travis and Sebastian are driving Matty and me nuts with their squabbling about it. I think you should consider hiring a new detective, Matty, or at least have a long talk with the one you've got."

"I'd vote for that." Luann took off her granny glasses and gazed at Matty and Gwen. "I'll always think of Elizabeth as my granddaughter, but I'd like to know if it's official or not."

"We'd all like to know," Matty said. "I think you'd like to know, too, wouldn't you, Shelby?" she added softly.

Shelby glanced up and her cheeks felt hot, but she looked bravely into Matty's blue eyes. Sebastian's wife missed nothing. "Well, sure, for Boone's sake," she said.

"And what about your own?" Matty asked.

"Uh, I think it would be premature to—"

"Hey." Gwen joined the discussion, reaching over to put her hand on Shelby's arm. "Don't feel like the Lone Ranger, hon. Matty and I have been where you are. It's hell when you're falling in love with a guy who won't commit because of some phantom woman who's running all over the countryside."

Shelby's cheeks warmed even more. "Oh, no. I'm not—"

Gwen squeezed her arm. "Sure you are. It's written all over your face when you look at that big cowboy. Right, Matty?"

"I'm afraid so."

Shelby was mortified. "Do you think he can tell?"

"Are you kidding?" Luann unwrapped a candy and popped it in her mouth. "He's a man, sweetie. You'd have to splash it across a billboard."

"I don't really want him to find out," Shelby said. "He already has so much to worry about, and I—"

"And you have a lot to worry about, too," Matty said. "Don't be too easy on the guy, or too hard on yourself. As Luann pointed out, he's a man. He probably has no idea what's good for him."

Gwen laughed. "Talk about stating the obvious. Of course he doesn't."

Matty picked up a piece of candy and stared at it for a while. Then she glanced at Gwen. "Maybe after you and Travis head off for your honeymoon, Sebastian and I can make a quick trip to Denver and talk to the folks at the agency." She looked across the table at Shelby. "Luann's going to be busy running the bed-and-breakfast for Gwen. How would you feel about baby-sitting for a couple of days? You and Boone?"

CHAOTIC THOUGHTS kept Shelby from sleeping very well that night. She had the definite feeling that Matty was matchmaking. Still, she tried not to dwell on the possibility that she and Boone would be able to spend more time alone together if Sebastian and Matty went to Denver and left them to watch the two kids. Sebastian might not even agree to the trip.

But he did. The next morning he and Travis were both at the breakfast table nursing a hangover when Matty informed them of Jessica's call. After Sebastian muttered a soft curse and massaged his temples, Matty proposed the quick trip to Denver. Then she suggested leaving Shelby and Boone in charge of the two children and the ranch while they were gone.

Sebastian looked at his wife and they seemed to exchange a signal of some sort. "Maybe that's a good idea," he said.

Elizabeth, who was in a playpen in the corner of the

kitchen, picked that moment to start fussing. Sebastian winced and closed his eyes. Josh had appointed himself in charge of the baby's happiness, and he clambered out of his chair to go check on her. In the process he knocked over his milk.

He stared at the milk, crestfallen. "Whoopsy-daisy," he said.

Shelby grabbed a sponge and started mopping. "That's okay, Josh."

"It was a accident!"

"Sure it was," Matty said, coming over to the table and smiling at Josh. "Go ahead and see about Elizabeth, honey. She likes it when you talk to her."

As Josh trotted over and began singing the ABC song to Elizabeth, Sebastian ran a hand over his face and sighed. "Yeah, Denver might be a very good idea."

"Denver?" Boone asked as he came in the back door. For the second night in a row, he'd bedded down in the barn.

Travis had spent the night, or what was left of it after the men had come home, on the living-room sofa. Bleary-eyed, he glanced over at Boone. "It seems they're appointing you and Shelby to baby-sit while they go to Denver and find out what's up with the private detective, who isn't finding diddly-squat."

"Oh."

Shelby concentrated on mopping up the milk and didn't look at him. As usual, his presence made her feel as if someone had touched her with a live electrical wire. She wondered if he was thinking the same thing that she was. In order to make sure she and the kids were safe, he'd have to sleep in the house instead of the barn. Matty had figured that out, of course.

"I guess that would be okay," Boone said.

His soft, gentle voice skipped along her nerves and her

knees grew weak. They would be alone in this house together for at least one night and maybe two. Well, alone except for the children. Children who slept at night. If Boone was in love with Jessica, then Shelby should probably stay away from him, even if he did end up sleeping right down the hall. Of course, he might not stay away from her....

"That security system Jim installed for the house is top-of-the-line," Sebastian said. "So you don't have to worry about—" He glanced significantly over at Josh. "You know what," he added.

"*Tell* me about that precious security system," Travis said. "I was afraid you and me were gonna end up sleeping on the porch last night when you were too ploughed to remember the code."

Sebastian eyed Travis across the table. "Oh, yeah? I distinctly heard you suggesting that we sleep out in the yard. You wanted to sleep under the stars like men, you said, to symbolize your last night of freedom. You were fried to your tonsils, hotshot."

"Was not."

"Were too."

Boone poured himself some coffee and sat down at the table. "Let me put it this way. The guys at the Buckskin will never forget the Daniels and Evans version of the theme song from *Bonanza*."

Sebastian frowned at Travis. "We didn't sing that last night, did we?"

"Nah," Travis said. "Ol' Boone's just making that up to harass us."

Boone chuckled. "You did more than sing it. There was a considerable amount of bumping and grinding going on."

Sebastian gave him a deadpan stare. "I refuse to believe that."

"Okay." Boone shrugged and took a drink of his coffee.

"Just don't be surprised if guys come up to you at the reception and ask how things are going out at the Ponderosa."

Matty laughed and pushed back her chair. "And I thought I was the boot-scootin' champion around here. Boone, would you like some breakfast? I can't seem to interest these two in my cooking, but you look like a man who could put away some bacon and eggs."

Travis groaned. "Just don't pass them under my nose."

"I'd love some breakfast," Boone said. "And if these cowboys can't take the heat, they can get out of the kitchen. What's the plan for today?"

Matty took a carton of eggs out of the refrigerator. "Shelby and I need to run into town for some reception goodies and take them over to Hawthorne House," she said. "If you three guys can handle it, I'd like you to watch the kids until we get back, which will be later this afternoon."

"Perfect," Boone said. "Then I can take Josh riding."

Josh leaped up from where he'd been crouching next to the playpen and ran over to Boone's chair. "Bob, too?"

Boone ruffled the little boy's hair. "Yeah, Bob, too."

The look he gave Josh made Shelby's heart turn over. Matty and Gwen were right. She was falling in love with Boone Connor.

AROUND THREE that afternoon, Shelby followed Matty through the front door of the ranch house. They were greeted with the sound of male voices raised in heated debate. Shelby figured out the noise was coming from Elizabeth's room after she heard a few baby chortles mixed in with the argument in progress.

"You didn't tell him to wipe from front to back, hotshot!" Sebastian said.

"That's because I was so busy keeping you from knocking over the baby oil!" Travis said. "You keep elbowing your way in there, because of course *nobody* does this as good as you, and now—"

"Will you two cowpokes back the heck off?" Boone sounded more impatient than Shelby had ever heard him. "No wonder I can't get the hang of this! It's as crowded as a bucking chute in here. And where's the blasted diaper?"

"I gots it!" Josh piped up. "Whoops. The tape comed off. It was a accident!"

Matty turned to Shelby and grinned. "It figures. Chaos."

"Oh, *man*." Sebastian's complaint floated down the hall. "This is the bad kind of diaper. Who bought these losers, as if I didn't know?"

"*I* did," Travis said, "and you can quit your bellyaching, because they're more absorbent. The kind *you* buy leak like a sieve. See? Right here it says—"

"My kind does not leak, and this kind has bad tape!"

"So you're starting me out with substandard equipment?" Boone asked. "What kind of outfit are you saddle tramps running, anyway?"

Shelby put her hand over her mouth to stifle a giggle.

"Come on." Matty beckoned to her and crept toward the hall. "This should be worth the price of admission."

Shelby followed Matty as the diaper argument continued. When she peered in the room, she had to press her lips together to keep from laughing out loud. Their backs to the door, all three cowboys jostled for position around the changing table, completely blocking any view of the baby. Josh bounced around behind them, jumping up every few seconds as he tried to see what was going on.

"No, don't do it that way," Sebastian said. "Here. Let me—"

"Get your mitts off her." Boone batted Sebastian's hand away.

"She likes it if you make faces at her while you're changing her," Travis said. "Don't you, Lizzy?"

"Don't be distracting her, Travis!" Boone said. "I've just about got this thingamajig—"

"She likes my singing better," Sebastian said.

"Don't you wish!" Travis said. "Watch this. Stick out your tongue, Lizzy. Like this. Thata-girl."

"She also likes her monkey Bruce." Sebastian waggled the sock monkey over the changing table. "Here's Brucey, Elizabeth!"

"Will you *move over?*" Boone sounded as if he was at the end of his rope. "There! Got the diaper on, no thanks to you morons. Now what are we putting on her?"

"I don't gots diapers anymore!" Josh proclaimed, hopping up and down. "I'm a big boy. Can I throw the diaper away? Can I? I wanna slam-dunk it."

Sebastian reached up to a shelf above the changing table where baby clothes were folded in neat stacks. "Put this on her." He shoved a red-and-white-ruffled outfit at Boone.

"No, not that." Travis took down something else. "This yellow terry job. We gotta feed her, don't forget, before the women get home. Matty won't like it if we get that ruffled thing all gucked up."

"I wanna slam-dunk the diaper," Josh repeated, leaping up and down.

"Speaking of the women," Sebastian said, "I sure do like Shelby, Boone."

Shelby's smile faded and she tensed.

"Me, too," Travis said.

"Me, too!" Josh announced.

"I like her, too," Boone said quietly, "but—"

"But nothing, man," Travis said. "Don't be an idiot."

Shelby's face grew hot, but when Matty quietly put a hand on her arm and tried to draw her back down the hall, she resisted. She wanted to know what Boone had to say about her when she wasn't around, although of course they'd all be careful, with Josh right there.

"Travis is right for once," Sebastian said. "And for some reason she seems to like you, too, even considering you're as stubborn as they come. Are you going to be dumb enough to louse this up?"

Shelby held her breath as her heart hammered in antici-pation of Boone's answer.

"Yeah, I probably am," Boone said.

Shelby's heart dropped to her toes. This time, when Matty tugged on her arm, she retreated with her, battling tears all the way.

When they were halfway back down the hall, Matty gave her a quick hug. "Hang in there," she murmured. "He'll come around."

Shelby didn't trust herself to speak, so she nodded.

"Come on, let's break up that party," Matty said softly. Then she raised her voice. "Hey, guys, we're home!" She started back down the hall, and unless Shelby wanted to look like a coward, she had no choice but to follow.

Sebastian spun around toward the doorway, the ruffled outfit still in one hand. "Matty!" He glanced guiltily at Shelby. "When did you two get back?"

"Just now," Matty said.

"Shebby!" Josh ran toward Shelby and threw his arms around her legs. "We rided the horsies!" He gazed up at her, his face alight with happiness. "Me and Bob and Boone! We went round and round and round and—"

"Sounds great." Forcing a smile, she leaned down to give him a hug.

"Time's getting short," Matty said to Sebastian. "Maybe you guys should go get cleaned up and into your duds while Shelby and I feed the kids."

164   *Boone's Bounty*

"Yes, ma'am," Sebastian said. "Come on, bridegroom. You, too, Boone."

Boone hoisted Elizabeth into his arms and turned to Matty, but instead of holding the baby out so Matty could take her, he kept her close against his chest.

Heartsick, Shelby took in the sight of Boone holding that sweet little girl. He glanced over at Shelby and his eyes shone with a gentle light as he stroked Elizabeth's downy hair with one big hand. His whole manner had changed from tentative to possessive. Shelby realized that while she'd been in town with Matty, Boone had staked his claim to his daughter. And it looked as if he had no room left in his heart for Shelby.

He turned toward Matty. "If it's all the same to you," he said, "I'd like to feed her."

13

CANDLELIGHT WEDDINGS sure made a church look cozy, Boone thought as he stood next to Sebastian at the altar. While the minister, Pete McDowell, talked about the holy state of matrimony, Boone congratulated himself on making it to Colorado in time. He wouldn't have wanted to miss seeing Travis and Gwen hitched, and besides, he balanced out the wedding party.

Gwen had decided to challenge tradition and had asked Luann to stand up with her, along with Matty. That way Luann could hold Elizabeth, which had seemed the best way to get the baby into the ceremony. Elizabeth was becoming quite a handful, and she might have tried to climb out of the buggy they'd used for Matty and Sebastian's wedding. If Boone hadn't been around, Luann would have had to walk back down the aisle by herself.

He still had trouble believing that Travis was really tying the knot. Apparently the women in the congregation had trouble believing it, too. Boone saw many a young lady sniffling into her handkerchief, and Boone didn't think they were crying for joy.

Boone's gaze moved over the crowd and came to rest again on the face that held the most interest for him tonight. Shelby sat on the end of a pew, near enough to a flickering candle that the light sparkled on the tears she bravely blinked away. He hadn't considered how tough this celebration would be on her. She was still grieving for her family, and the warm, happy scene probably reminded her of how alone she was except for the little boy snuggled next to her, his hair slicked back and his eyes wide. Boone's chest grew tight and his arms ached with the urge to comfort her.

Matty had loaned Shelby a pale blue dress, and when she'd come out into the ranch-house living room wearing it, Boone had been so dazzled he hadn't been able to think of anything to say. Josh had told her she looked "like a princess." She'd glanced uncertainly at Boone, as if wanting his opinion. "You look nice" had been the best he could do. Lame, totally lame.

But maybe it was good that he hadn't paid her much of a compliment. He had no business getting her hopes up about him. He'd made a huge mistake with that incident in the barn and now this baby-sitting assignment was going to be a real test of his ability to stay away from her.

All he wanted to do was help and protect her, but instead he seemed to be making her miserable. Correction—he was making them *both* miserable, because after those moments in the barn, all he could think about was holding her like that again.

As Pete McDowell moved into the vows portion of the ceremony, Boone glanced over at Gwen. He didn't know much about women's clothes, but he could tell she'd gone for the old-fashioned look, with lots of ivory lace and little pearls everywhere. It was an impressive outfit, but the rapture on her face completely outshone the dress and veil.

Boone's heart twisted as he realized it was the kind of expression he longed to see on Shelby's face. Lord help him, he wanted to be standing at this altar with Shelby. And because of Elizabeth, he had no right.

FOR JOSH'S SAKE, Shelby kept a tight grip on her emotions during the ceremony. When the tears came, she whisked them quickly away. Concentrating on Boone helped keep her strong. His tux was too small, which only emphasized what a giant of a man he was. He appeared gorgeously serious and forbidding standing up there. Unshakable. Ah, but he wasn't. She'd seen him come undone.

No one observing Boone looking so dignified in his elegant tie and tails would ever guess what he'd been doing with her twenty-four hours ago. Her body warmed to the memory of how he'd kissed her...everywhere. In spite of what he'd said to his friends this afternoon, he hadn't been so cavalier when he held her in his arms. In fact, she'd caused this rock of a man to go a little crazy. She'd hold onto that knowledge.

Boone might never belong to her, but she got under his skin, and that was nice to know. He'd been thinking about her, she could tell. His gaze had touched hers more than once. Knowing him, he was probably wrestling with the question of how he'd get through baby-sitting without giving in to temptation.

She was sure he didn't want to succumb, because his moral code was a few notches above that of most men. Shelby didn't want him to go against that code if he would think less of himself as a result, but oh, how she longed for a night of loving Boone.

Judging from the experience in the barn, she could probably override his control and seduce him. But she'd seen how he beat himself up over the possibility that he'd inappropriately made love to Jessica. No matter how satisfying loving Boone might be, Shelby didn't want to add another burden to his conscience. Boone was the sort to carry that burden to his grave. So it was settled. They wouldn't make love while Matty and Sebastian were gone.

Boone glanced in her direction again, and his green eyes

glowed with an intensity that threatened to melt all her good intentions.

"Shebby," Josh whispered. "Gwen and Travis are kissing in front of all the peoples!"

"That's because they're married now, sweetheart," Shelby murmured, still holding Boone's gaze. Was it only sexual desire she saw there, or something more lasting?

Then the minister presented the newly married couple, and the congregation burst into applause. Boone looked away, and Shelby decided wishful thinking was making her imagine things. Boone might want her, but he wasn't happy about it.

FATE HAD SMILED on him, Mason decided as he slipped quietly out of the yard adjacent to Hawthorne House where the wedding reception was in full swing. Thanks to his excellent reconnaissance skills, he'd found out exactly what he needed to know by listening in on a few conversations.

He left the music and laughter and twinkling lights behind as he started the trek back to his campsite outside of town. Let the wedding guests enjoy themselves. The fun and games would be over soon enough.

Beginning tomorrow night, Shelby and the kid would be alone at the ranch except for one big, dumb cowboy and a little baby. With the element of surprise, Mason figured he could get his kid back. Maybe in the process he'd even put a nice little scare into Shelby, so she'd understand who she was messing with.

This whole operation was right on track. With Huerfano being a tourist town, he'd been able to locate a campground where he could keep a low profile. Although the wedding had seemed like a nuisance at first, he'd quickly realized he could use the time during the ceremony to check out the security system at the ranch.

It was nothing he couldn't get around. His crummy part-time job selling home-security systems had come in handy, after all. He might not have sold anything, but he'd learned a hell of a lot about how most systems worked.

He was good at this kind of mission, though, damn good. He'd have made a fine Navy SEAL, too, if the brass hadn't had it in for him. Once he got his hands on the kid and he was assured of a steady supply of money, he'd give up the security-systems racket and see what he could find that would make better use of his skills, something that would be fun.

There had to be people out there who would pay for his natural talent in espionage, people with deep pockets who didn't care to advertise in the Help Wanted section of the newspaper. A couple of his buddies had hinted they had contacts, but he'd never felt he had the financial freedom to try a risky new venture like that. But now—now anything was possible.

LATE THE FOLLOWING afternoon Shelby stirred a pot of beef stew in between setting the table for dinner and glancing out the window to catch a glimpse of Boone. He was doing the evening chores with Elizabeth in a carrier strapped to his back. Josh and both dogs stayed right at his heels.

Matty and Sebastian had left about lunchtime for Denver, and Boone had started immediately on the long-overdue job of shoeing Sebastian and Matty's horses. Shelby had kept Elizabeth and Josh up at the house, figuring they shouldn't be underfoot while Boone was working.

As dinnertime approached, though, Boone had returned from the barn and volunteered to take both kids so she could fix the meal without being constantly interrupted. It was a kind gesture, but Shelby could tell from the way he was interacting with both Elizabeth and Josh that he relished being with them.

She watched him now as he crouched down to look at some treasure Josh had found. It was probably only a stone that had caught the little boy's eye, but Boone examined it as if Josh had discovered the Hope diamond. Both dogs came over to look, too, wagging their tails and trying to lick Josh's face.

Then from her perch in the carrier Elizabeth made a grab for Boone's hat. He ended up taking it off and putting it on Josh, who wore it as if he'd been crowned King of England, even though it came down over his ears and he could barely see out from under the brim.

The faint scent of scorched stew pulled Shelby away from the window. She turned down the flame under the burner and vowed to pay more attention to her job, but her mind was filled with images of Boone, Elizabeth and Josh. Her own experience didn't give her much of a yardstick concerning family men, but even she could see that Boone would make a wonderful husband and father.

Minutes later Boone, Josh and Elizabeth came through the back door, followed by Fleafarm and Sadie. Once Boone was inside, he turned and set the security alarm. Shelby didn't know much about alarms, but this seemed like a good one. She doubted it was necessary, though. It was hard to believe Mason had tracked her to this remote ranch, but with the alarm, the dogs and Boone, she felt quite safe.

"Look, Shebby!" Josh held out his treasure, a baseball-sized rock flecked with bits of gold. "Iron pie-bite!"

"*Pyrite*," Boone corrected gently.

"Yep," Josh said happily. "Looks like gold, huh? Me and Bob found it. Maybe they really gots gold around here!"

Shelby admired the sparkling rock. "You never know. It

sure is pretty, though. Better go put it in a safe place in your room. Then go wash your hands. We're ready to eat."

"'Kay!" Josh started out of the kitchen, his free hand clapped over Boone's hat to keep it from falling off.

"And maybe you'd better give that hat back," Shelby said.

Josh turned and peered up from under the wide brim. "Do I hafta?"

"Tell you what, Josh," Boone said. "You can wear it until you go to bed tonight. Then tomorrow we'll take a run into town and find one that fits you a little better."

"This one fits real good," Josh insisted.

"It's not bad," Boone said, obviously trying not to smile, "but I think we can do better. And besides, you need boots. We'll pick those up tomorrow, too."

Josh grinned. "*Okay!*" He started to run out of the room.

"Walk," Shelby called after him. Then she turned to Boone. "Let me take that little papoose so you can go wash up, too."

"Thanks." He turned his back and hunkered down slightly so she could lift the baby out of the carrier. "Dinner smells good."

"It's a pretty simple meal—one of Josh's favorites." She tried to ignore the excitement that always stirred in her when he stood this close.

"I like simple food the best." Boone moved his arm back right at the moment Shelby leaned forward to lift Elizabeth out, and he nudged her breast. "Sorry."

"No problem." Her breast tingled, and the feeling began to spread.

Boone moved away the minute she had Elizabeth free. He took off the carrier and propped it in the corner. He made a good show of looking nonchalant as he walked to the stove and lifted the lid on the beef stew. "Yum. I was practically raised on this stuff."

Then what this world needs is more beef stew, if it produces hunks like you, she thought. "I sure wasn't raised on it," she said. She propped Elizabeth in her high chair. "We had a cook who fixed nothing but gourmet, and I used to dread meals as a kid. I faked stomach flu whenever we had escargots. I don't want to put Josh through that." She fastened the high-chair tray securely in place.

When she looked up she caught Boone silently watching her, his gaze on the top button of her blouse. His glance moved to her face, and his green eyes were hot. The tension crackling between them nearly made her forget what else he'd been doing when she'd looked up. Then she realized he'd been massaging his shoulder, as if he had an injury of some kind.

"Are you okay?" she asked.

He broke eye contact. "Sure. Fine. Listen, why don't I check on Josh?" He left the room before she could question him further.

As she spooned up cereal and scooped it into Elizabeth's rosebud mouth, Shelby could hear Josh and Boone laughing and talking in the bathroom. She wondered how Josh would ever manage when he had to leave Boone.

The two of them apparently found a lot to talk about, and Shelby was nearly finished feeding Elizabeth when Boone returned carrying Josh piggyback.

"Boone told me about hats." Josh bounced along happily. "They gots beaver hats, and straw hats, but when you buy one, you gots to fix it so it gots *style*. Right, Boone?"

"Right."

Elizabeth chortled and held out her cereal-smeared hands toward Boone.

"My turn, Lizzie," Josh said, with a trace of possessiveness. "You gots your turn. Put me up higher, Boone! On your shoulders, okay?"

"Sure." Boone lifted Josh up and settled him over his shoulders.

If Shelby hadn't been watching so closely, she might have missed Boone's wince of pain. "You're hurt," she said.

"Nah. How do you like it up there, pardner?"

"I'm king of the whole wide world!" Josh said.

Shelby gave Elizabeth's face and hands a quick wipe and glanced back at Josh. "Time to get down, buckaroo," she said with a smile. "Dinner's ready."

"Aww." Josh stuck out his lower lip.

"Better listen to the lady," Boone said. "When it comes to chow-time, she's the boss." He set Josh back on his feet and repositioned the oversized hat. "Take a seat, cowboy. I'll help Shelby dish up."

"We'll see about that, Boone." Shelby stood, determined to find out if Boone was injured. "First, I want you to take off your shirt."

"What?" He stared at her.

"Go on, take it off. You said you're not hurt. Prove it to me."

He looked uncomfortable. "It's nothing. A little kick, is all. Then the carrier rubbed on the spot. But I'll be fine."

"I'm sure you will. Let me see."

Josh scrambled off his chair. "I wanna see."

"Hey, it's really nothing," Boone said. "Let's forget it."

She folded her arms and waited.

His green eyes grew soft and smoky. "Please."

She was no match for a look like that. When he gave her that kind of look she wanted to wrap her arms around him and lift her mouth for his kiss. She unfolded her arms and blew out a breath. "Okay, you win. Let's eat."

BOONE HOPED Shelby had forgotten about his shoulder in all the hubbub of dinner and starting the kids toward bed. While she read Josh a story, Boone let the dogs out for one last run. Standing on the porch waiting for them to come back, he assessed his shoulder by prodding it with the tips of his fingers.

He had a good-sized bruise there, and if he'd been alone, he would have taken time to put some ice on it. But doing that would bring attention to his injury. The bruise might upset Josh, for one thing. But the real danger was in letting Shelby get involved in nursing him.

The dogs loped back up to the porch and he went inside. The little kick of excitement in his stomach had to be ignored, he told himself. Nothing would happen between him and Shelby tonight. Absolutely nothing.

She didn't mention his shoulder again as they finished putting the kids to bed. He couldn't believe how much he loved taking care of Josh and Elizabeth, and how natural it seemed to be doing these chores with Shelby. The four of them were a great fit, with Josh taking the role of Elizabeth's older brother, and Elizabeth apparently happy to have Josh sleeping in the same room with her.

Josh needed a little calming down, but he agreed to go to bed once Boone reminded him that the sooner he went to sleep, the sooner morning would come and they could drive into town to shop for his hat and boots. Boone thought he was probably as excited about the prospect as Josh.

As a reminder of coming attractions, Boone left his hat on Josh's bedpost. After collecting good-night kisses from Boone and Shelby, Josh finally went to sleep clutching his "gold" rock in his hand.

Boone went out into the hallway and Shelby followed, closing the door partway after her.

"He's been in seventh heaven the past few days," she murmured. "Thank you for all the time you've given him."

"I've had fun." Boone glanced back at her. "He's a great kid." *And he's the perfect chaperone.* Boone felt the privacy of the narrow hallway closing in on him, creating feelings he had no business having about the woman so temptingly near. He wanted to push her against the wall, kiss her senseless, unbutton her blouse, her jeans....

This was the moment he'd been dreading, when the two of them had no distractions. The light in the hallway was dim, but he could still see her expression far too well. She was looking at him with way too much tenderness.

"I wonder what's on the tube tonight?" he said abruptly. He hardly ever watched TV, but suddenly it seemed like the best idea going. "Let's go see." He started down the hall toward the living room.

She caught his arm. "Boone, let me look at your shoulder."

He tensed as the pressure of her fingers sizzled along his nerve endings. He squelched the urge to jerk his arm away, although that might be the safest move. Trying for a cool attitude in spite of his blazing hormones, he looked down at her. "Never mind about the shoulder," he said. "I'm fine."

Her gaze was soft. The rest of her would be, too. So very, very soft. "I don't believe you," she said.

"You have to." His voice sounded like tires on gravel.

"Why?" She left her hand right where it was, lightly holding on to his arm.

Her touch felt like a branding iron, burning through the cotton of his shirt to singe the hair on his arms. He gritted his teeth against the urges washing over him, the need to once again explore her mouth, her breasts, the warm, moist place between her thighs. "Because I'm not taking off my shirt."

She swallowed. "If you think I'm trying to seduce you, I'm not. I'm just worried that you're hurt and you won't take care of yourself properly. I checked and there's a first-aid kit in the bathroom. I could—"

"I don't think so."

She gulped, but her chin lifted with determination and that crazy little ponytail she liked to wear on top of her head wiggled. "Boone, don't be stubborn. I wouldn't—"

"No, but I would." In a heartbeat. He could have her clothes off in ten seconds flat.

Wordlessly she gazed at him, a pulse beating in her throat.

His chest tightened with the effort not to pull her into his arms. "Move...move your hand. Please."

Her eyes still locked with his, she released her grip on his arm.

"Thank you." Summoning all his strength, he turned toward the living room.

"Are you in love with her?"

He paused. She must mean Jessica. He sensed that if he lied and said he was, that she would back off and they'd both be saved.

"It's okay if you are," she said in a small voice. "And I don't think any less of you for what happened in the barn. I'm sure when a man is...frustrated, his control can snap. I was available. And you're only human."

He groaned and leaned a hand against the wall. He didn't want her thinking he'd only used her as a sexual outlet.

"I wonder if she realizes how lucky she is," Shelby whispered. "Well, good night, Boone. And please put something on that shoulder before you go to bed."

"I don't love Jessica." The words just came out. He hadn't even realized what he'd been about to say, only that he couldn't let her believe herself only a handy convenience for him.

"You...don't?"

He shook his head, still not trusting himself to look at her. "That's why what I did, getting her pregnant, was so wrong."

"You really don't love her?" Shelby's voice came from right beside him. "Or are you just saying that because she doesn't love you back?"

He straightened and faced her. If only he had the strength to let her believe all the hogwash she'd made up about his situation, he'd spare himself and her a lot of grief. But then she'd think that whole episode in the barn had nothing to do with her, and everything to do with him missing the lady in his life. He couldn't have Shelby, who meant so much to him, thinking something like that.

Shelby's eyes glowed with feeling. "I can't imagine why she wouldn't love you back. You're everything any woman could want."

He wished he could be worthy of her high opinion. Looking at her angel's face, he could barely breathe, let along talk. But he had to try. "Jessica and I are just friends. We've never been more than friends."

"But...Matty said..." She hesitated.

His face grew hot at the idea Matty had been talking about him to Shelby. Still, he had to know. "Matty said what?"

"That there was someone, someone you cared about, and it didn't turn out well."

"There was." And at the moment he couldn't imagine why he'd ever pined away for Darlene. She didn't hold a candle to Shelby.

"So are you still in love with *her?*"

"No." Amazingly, it was true. And he'd be happier about it if he hadn't jumped from the frying pan into the fire.

"Then you're not in love with anybody?"

He gazed down at her, his heart pounding. "I didn't say that."

14

SHELBY FELT UNSTEADY and shivery. A surge of heat followed, then shivers shook her again as Boone's reply echoed in her head. He was looking at her now with the same intensity he had during the wedding ceremony. Possibilities she'd never allowed herself to dream of seemed suddenly within reach.

But this wasn't the most forthcoming man in the world. She had to be courageous and risk rejection in order to make sure she understood him. "What are you saying, Boone?"

"I don't have a damn right to say anything." But his eyes still blazed with green fire.

The message in those eyes seemed blatantly clear. She began to quiver with anticipation. Embarrassed by how shaky she felt, she put both hands behind her back and leaned her shoulders against the wall, pretending to be casual but desperately needing the wall for support. "I'm not sure I understand what you mean."

"Shelby." His voice sounded strained. "Don't do that."

"Do what?"

"Lean like that." His gaze lingered on her breasts, and his breathing grew ragged.

She realized that her attempt to be casual had resulted in her breasts thrusting out and up in what looked like an invitation to touch. She hadn't done it deliberately, but as she noticed his agitation and the bulge in his jeans, her shakes began to disappear.

In the process she discovered something very wicked about herself. Now that he'd said he wasn't in love with someone else and had come close to admitting he might be in love with her, she was ready to play on his weakness for her body.

Her careful, deep breath strained the buttons on her blouse. "Why, does it bother you?"

He looked like a man about to break. "You know it does. And I can't—I have nothing to offer you."

"Except what you gave me the other night in the barn?"

The heat in his eyes increased by several degrees. "Damn it. Don't remind me of that."

"Do I have to remind you?" she asked in a low voice. "Or is it what you think about constantly?"

He stepped closer. "I think about it constantly," he said. Flattening his palms against the wall, he stared down at her. His warm breath feathered her face. "Constantly."

Her heartbeat sounded a deep and frantic rhythm in her ears. "Me, too," she whispered.

"Tell me to go away, Shelby." His attention became fixed on her mouth. "For God's sake, don't look so ready to be kissed. You're driving me crazy, you know that?"

"I know." Meeting the challenge in his eyes, she moistened her lips, parted them, teased him with a sultry look. "Drive me crazy, too, Boone. One more time."

"I have to kiss you. But that's it. Nothing else."

She started to put her arms around his neck.

"No," he whispered, leaning down. "Don't touch me. Just let me kiss you. One kiss." His palms still braced against the wall, he leaned down and touched his mouth to hers. He began with slow, sensuous nibbles, as if her lips were a sugary treat he wanted to make last a long time.

"Your mouth is so...ripe," he murmured. He raked her

bottom lip gently between his teeth. "I want to gobble you up."

"I want you to. I want you to kiss me all over."

His quiet moan spoke of his frustration. "I can't risk that again. But I can do this." As if he had forever, he outlined her entire mouth with languorous flicks of his tongue. And although his only point of contact was her mouth, he did indeed drive her crazy. He was making love to her mouth, she realized, and this was foreplay.

When she was gasping, nearly begging for a more full-bodied kiss, he gradually dipped his tongue deeper and settled his lips more firmly over hers. Her heart thundered as he stroked the inside of her mouth. The motion blended with memory, as her body recalled the satisfaction he'd brought her once before with that wonderful tongue. The throbbing core of her moistened in readiness.

As his tongue continued to caress her, the rhythmic sensation spiraled downward. An insistent tension coiled ever tighter between her thighs. Clenching her fists at her sides, she moaned and opened her mouth wider, wanting to be ravished. He continued to caress only her hot mouth as he plunged deep, his breath coming fast.

Her nipples tightened and thrust against her blouse. She wanted him to cup and stroke her there, yet still he kept his palms flat against the wall. The ache pulsed ever stronger between her thighs. She wanted him there, as well—caressing, kissing, thrusting. At last the force of her need tricked her, guiding her to imagine him touching her everywhere, and there, especially *there*. As he kissed her with passionate abandon, she arched away from the wall. Her shuddering climax took her by storm.

He caught her in his strong arms before she crumpled to the floor. "Shelby," he murmured against her cheek as he gathered her up and carried her toward her room. "Oh, Shelby, sweetheart."

She struggled for breath. "Come to bed with me," she begged.

His voice rasped in the stillness. "It's not...a good idea."

"Do it anyway."

He carried her into her bedroom. "No. I—" In the dark he tripped against Sebastian's office chair and sent it rolling across the floor. It was a testament to his strength that he stayed upright and didn't drop her. "I'm leaving you here. Lock the door." He deposited her on the daybed.

Sitting up immediately, she reached over and snagged his belt buckle before he could turn away. "Oh, no, you don't."

"Let go, Shelby." He sounded as if he might strangle on the words as he fought a desperate battle between desire and conscience.

She didn't let go. She'd made it this far past his natural barriers, and retreat wasn't an option. He wouldn't have birth control with him, so she had to find another way to show him what he would be missing if he walked out that door. Grasping the tab on his zipper, she pulled it firmly down.

He clearly hadn't expected her to be so bold, judging from his quick gasp. Before he could recover enough to grab her wrists and stop her, she slipped her hand inside and stroked the solid length of him.

He groaned and tried to manacle her wrists in his long fingers. "No," he whispered.

"Yes. Let me love you," she murmured. She pulled her hand away and her searching fingers found the opening in his briefs, caressing the hot, smooth skin of his erect penis. "Please. Let me love you before you go."

"It's not right." But his protest was weaker, the grip on her one wrist not nearly so tight.

Had there been more light in the room, he never would have let her touch him like this, she thought. Instinctively she knew he wasn't a man who freely opened himself to such intimacies. Yet here, in the dark, after the amazing kiss they'd shared, his defenses were down. He might, just might, give in to the fantasy.

"You've been so good to me," she said softly. "Let me make you feel good, too."

The moan deep in his throat could have been either protest or permission. She took it for permission. Slowly she eased her hand inside his briefs and grasped him gently. He was so large her fingers couldn't complete the circle.

Heart pounding from the discovery of his incredible girth, she explored his length and grew dizzy imagining so much man deep inside her. She would know that thrill, too, but first she needed to stake her claim.

The sound of his rapid breathing filled the small room, brushed by a faint glow of light from the hall, as she nudged his erection free of the cotton material. With a sigh of surrender he released her wrist. Triumph surged through her as she took him in both hands.

She could feel the blood pounding through the impressive length beneath her fingers. As she ran her hands slowly upward, his penis twitched in reaction. Then, as she eased her grip and slid her hands back down, she leaned forward and kissed the moist tip. His whole body trembled, like the quaking of a giant tree about to topple to the forest floor.

A sense of power encouraged her to taunt him even more. She swirled her tongue in a lazy motion around the slight ridge just below the tip, and he trembled again. Then she placed her mouth against the velvet surface, and in a pace designed to drive him wild, she began to draw him in.

He gasped for breath. And gradually, tentatively, his big hands cupped the back of her head, his thumbs resting against her temples. Whether his touch was meant to restrain or encourage her, she wasn't sure. But when he applied a slight pressure she knew that Boone, who never asked for anything, was asking now. His pride and shyness were being consumed by fiery need.

She could not take all of him, and he seemed to hang onto enough of his sanity to know that. But his passiveness slipped away as he began to thrust gently yet eagerly into her mouth. With a broken cry his fingers tightened against her scalp, and the salty rush of his climax flavored her tongue.

BOONE SANK to his knees in front of Shelby. He longed to shower her with diamonds, yet all he could give was a kiss filled with awe and tenderness. The taste of him remained on her lips, and he was humbled once again by her generosity. And still aroused. He'd never guessed that this angelic woman would be so daring with a man. The room was filled with the erotic scent of passion, his and hers.

She wanted him still. He could tell from the way she opened to his kiss. And he, too, wanted more, wanted to find out if she would become a wild creature when he pushed deep inside her. She was so small. He would have to be careful with her—if she would let him be careful. Already his penis was stirring at the thought of being enclosed by that hot, tight little body.

Lifting his mouth from hers, he tilted her head back and gazed into her shadowed eyes. His voice was husky with an emotion he hadn't expected to feel again for a long time, if ever. "We're not finished, are we?"

"No," she murmured.

He brushed his thumbs across her cheeks. "Nothing's changed. I still have a duty to Jessica. And the baby."

"You do," she agreed, her voice low and rich with desire. "But everything's changed."

He took a shaky breath. "Maybe."

"If you don't know it yet..." She pressed her forefinger against his bottom lip before sliding it smoothly into his mouth. "You will when you're deep inside me."

The surge of lust came like a blow to the gut. No matter what had just happened between them, he wanted her so fiercely that he nearly pushed her to the mattress then and there.

But before he could decide his next move, Josh's small voice carried down the hall.

"Shebby?" he called plaintively. "Bob, he had a bad dream."

"I'd better go," she said.

He stood and zipped his pants. Then he stepped aside to let her pass.

She rose on tiptoe and gave him a quick kiss. "I'll be back."

Such a simple statement, but it made his heart thunder. "Do you want me to see if I can find some con—"

"*Yes.*" Tucking in her blouse, she hurried out the door.

Moments later, as he searched Sebastian and Matty's bathroom cupboards, he listened to the muted sounds of Shelby talking to Josh. His heart wrenched as he faced the truth. Both of them had become so much a part of him that he might not survive without them. But what if Jessica wanted marriage? After what he'd done, he couldn't refuse her anything.

Well, if Jessica wanted marriage, he'd give it to her. And if that happened, he would never hold Shelby in his arms again.

Jessica could return any time. Tomorrow, in fact. Matty

had said she'd sounded happy to know that he was at the ranch. Tonight could be all he and Shelby would ever have.

He found the condoms. Carrying the box, he made a last tour of the house, shutting off lights and double-checking locks. The alarm was activated and the dogs lay sleeping in Josh and Elizabeth's room. It should be enough, but if not, he'd be here, ready to protect those he loved. And that was exactly what he felt for the three people in this house. Might as well be honest with himself. He'd fallen hard for each of them.

Finally he returned to the guest room and wondered whether he should undress. No. But he could at least take off his boots. He sat on Sebastian's desk chair to pull them off. When he was finished he impulsively leaned over and switched on the antique banker's lamp with the green glass shade. The light cast a soft circle of light over the rumpled daybed.

Good, thought Boone. He and Shelby had spent enough time in darkness. If this could be his only night with Shelby, he wanted to see everything. Most of all he wanted to be able to look into her eyes as he undressed her, to watch those blue eyes sparkle with excitement as he stroked her soft skin, and finally, to see them glow with passion as he pushed slowly, tenderly inside her.

MASON LOWERED his night-vision binoculars. At last his targets were moving toward bedtime. The lights were out in the front of the house, but one had flicked on in a back room. From the pattern of lights he'd figured out where Josh must be sleeping. That light had blinked out an hour ago, sometime around eight.

He could imagine what might be going on in the room with the light. And he figured it would work to his advantage. He hoped the bitch would wear that cowboy out.

Heavy-duty sex made a guy sleep like the dead, which was exactly how Mason would like that big lug to sleep tonight. Shelby was doing Mason a favor without even knowing it.

Once the light went out, Mason planned to give them another couple of hours to finish their hanky-panky and fall asleep. Then he'd make his move. First he'd disengage the alarm. As for the dogs, the big cowboy had played into his hands by letting the pooches out right on schedule.

Mason had watched through his binoculars as those dumb canines had wolfed down the hamburger he'd left on the ground where they'd be sure and find it. The tranquilizer buried inside the patties would keep them out of the action until morning.

He could smell success, and damned if it wouldn't be sweeter than going to bed with a willing virgin. The operation seemed almost too easy, but that was because, as usual, people had underestimated Mason Fowler. And by the time they realized their mistake, it would be too late.

BOONE HAD JUST thrown back the covers on the bed when Shelby came into the room. She reappeared so silently that only his sharpened sense of her let him know she was there. He turned to look at her, taking his time, memorizing the way she looked now and imagining how she'd look as he gradually took off her clothes. He didn't plan to rush the process this time.

When he noticed that she'd taken off her shoes and stood there in her socks, he realized why he hadn't heard her come in. So she'd decided to start by taking off her shoes, too, he thought with an inward smile. He loved the idea that she was so eager for him.

But as she stood in the doorway, color tinged her cheeks. For a woman who had acted so boldly not long ago, she seemed hesitant, almost shy.

"Josh had some trouble going back to sleep." She swallowed and made a nervous gesture with her hand. "And I...I checked on Elizabeth, too. She's fine."

"Good. Thank you." He thought of what a wonderful mother Shelby would make. She deserved a baby of her own. He pictured her growing round, her belly becoming almost as big as she was. And he wanted to be the one to plant the seed.

Her cheeks still glowing a rosy pink, she glanced back at the door. "I guess we should close that."

"Yes."

She turned and closed the door with a soft click. Then she faced him again. Like a wild thing struck with curiosity, she slowly ventured farther into the room. He waited, afraid she'd changed her mind and couldn't think how to tell him.

When she hesitated and rested her hand on the desk, his fear grew. "You know, it's easier when you're caught up in the moment," she said, running her finger back and forth along the edge of the desk. Then she cleared her throat. "Now that we've been interrupted, I'm not sure what to do next, Boone."

Pain knifed through him. But if she'd reconsidered, he'd honor that. "You've changed your mind?"

She shook her head. "Oh, no."

Thank God. "Then—"

"My rhythm's messed up, is all. I don't know whether to throw myself into your arms, or do a sexy striptease, or take *your* clothes off, or—"

"Then let me decide," he said with a small smile and a huge feeling of relief. If that was all that was bothering her, he could take care of it. He wanted to take care of it, in fact. He held out his hand.

Holding his gaze, she came toward him and put her hand

in his. "I noticed you turned on the light," she said in a breathy voice.

"Yes." His hand dwarfed hers. He brought it to his lips, turned it palm up and placed a kiss there. "You're so small and delicate," he murmured, tracing the shallow creases in her palm. He glanced into her eyes. "Are you afraid? Because I'm so big?"

"No." Her voice had become almost a whisper.

He unfastened the button at her wrist. "You know I'll be careful."

"Yes, I know."

Easing her sleeve back, he slowly kissed his way from the pulse at her wrist to the inside of her elbow. Along the journey he savored the satiny feel of her pale skin and the almost innocent scent of soap and flowers. His angel, who could seem so fragile one minute and so sexually daring the next. She made his head spin.

As he trailed his tongue along the return path to her wrist, she sighed. "That's why I'm not afraid," she murmured. "You are so..." She paused as he relinquished one hand and took the other, unfastening the button there. When he placed his lips against the inside of her other wrist, she sighed again. "So gentle."

He hoped he could live up to that. They were only beginning, and already fine tremors passed relentlessly through him, and beneath his jeans he was hard and hot. Unbuttoning the front of her blouse should have taken only one hand, but desire affected his coordination and he needed two. Gradually the placket gapped open, revealing the lacy cups of her bra. She'd begun breathing faster, and her breasts, cradled in white lace, quivered in response. He licked dry lips.

The light in the barn hadn't been very good. He hadn't been able to see clearly what he'd enjoyed that night, but he would take the time to see now. Pulling the tails of her blouse from the waistband of her jeans, he continued to watch the rapid rise and fall of her breasts as he pushed the blouse off her shoulders. It slid down her arms and whispered to the floor.

His heart hammered in anticipation as he reached behind her back and unfastened the hooks of her bra. Lifting it by the straps, he pulled it down, and nearly forgot to breathe. He'd remembered the heart-stopping fullness of her breasts and how they'd seemed even fuller contrasted with her small rib cage and narrow waist.

But colors had been muted in the barn. He hadn't seen the delicate tracing of blue veins, or that her nipples were such a tender shade of rose, a shade that deepened as he gazed. The tips grew more erect with each breath she took, and he remembered this was a woman who could climax with only a kiss.

He looked into her eyes and the blue sparkle had turned to intense navy. Cupping a breast in each hand, he shuddered at the delicious weight filling his palms. He had big hands, yet she nearly overflowed his grasp. Just by smoothing his thumbs over her taut nipples, he made her gasp. Instinctively he realized that if he suckled her, even for a moment, she could erupt.

And he didn't want that. Not yet. Instead he leaned down, softly kissed each raspberry tip, and released those heavenly breasts. Her jeans came next, and although he lectured himself to go slow, he took them off much too fast. But he wanted...oh, how he wanted to discover what he'd suspected, that her panties were drenched and fragrant with passion.

With one hand behind her nape, he watched her expression as he spread his hand and placed it firmly against the wet cotton panel between her thighs. A flame leaped in her eyes. He slipped his hand inside her panties and found her slick and hot to the touch.

The fire burned brighter in her eyes, and then she blushed again. Her lashes fluttered down. "You must think I'm..."

"Wonderful?"

"Oversexed."

His hand stilled. The thought had never occurred to him. He'd simply been grateful for her response.

"But I'm not usually so...excitable."

An emotion stronger than gratitude blossomed in him. "You're not?"

She opened her eyes and looked up at him. Then she shook her head.

"Oh, Shelby." Postponing his intimate caress, he cradled her face in both hands and kissed her, putting all that he didn't know how to say into that kiss.

His mouth was tender and reverent against hers. *I love you.* But those were words best not spoken. Not when his future was so uncertain.

Her lips were incredibly sweet. He could be content with this.... But no sooner had the thought come than he knew it was a lie. His fingers were still damp from his intimate caress. As he stroked her cheek, he breathed in the aroma of her passion. The maddeningly erotic scent worked on him until tenderness became urgency and urgency became frenzy. He backed her toward the bed.

If she hadn't matched him in eagerness, he might have regained control, but she fumbled with his shirt buttons and tore at his belt buckle. She had his jeans open before she tumbled backward onto the mattress. Frantic now, he finished the job, nearly groaning in relief as he stepped out of the jeans and briefs and his erection sprang free. By the time he'd grabbed a condom, ripped open the package and rolled it on, she'd torn off her panties and lay waiting for him.

His hungry gaze roamed over the intoxicating sight of her, all flushed and panting and ready. So ready. The bed was short and narrow, but it would have to do. He put a knee between her thighs, his eyes fixed on hers. Despite the forces raging in him, he paused. Now was the time to be careful. Now was the moment they would remember forever, and he wanted it to be right.

"Hurry," she whispered, "I want you so much I feel like I might faint."

"Me, too. But I'm not going to hurry."

"*Boone.*"

"Bend your knees," he murmured.

She drew her knees up.

Bracing a hand on either side of her, he leaned forward and lowered his head to brush her mouth with his. His heart beat like a crazed drummer, yet he had to maintain control. "Don't let me hurt you," he said. "Stop me if I'm hurting you." He slid one hand between her thighs and stroked her damp curls. "Promise me."

"I promise." She gasped as he pressed two fingers deep inside.

"Too much?"

"Not enough," she said, taunting him.

But he knew she was small, knew he would stretch her to her limits. Sitting back on his heels, he cradled a smooth thigh in each hand and guided her knees back and apart. His breath caught. There was the rosy entrance to heaven, glistening and waiting for him.

He leaned forward again, watching her eyes. Always watching her eyes as he slipped his throbbing penis just inside. There. That was the emotion he wanted to see in those blue eyes. He had no right to claim her, but it was all he wanted to do. She was the mate he'd waited a lifetime to find. He trembled as he restrained the overwhelming urge to ram deep.

"Good," she whispered.

Concentrating on the glow in her eyes, he pushed further in. Perfection. His heart ached for what they could have, if only...

A fraction more. He'd had no idea of the ecstasy of being tightly enclosed in her hot sheath. The friction was incredible, and in no time he was balanced on the edge of an orgasm. Or maybe it was more than the friction that had created this powerful need for release. He longed to empty himself in her, in Shelby. To create a child. Dizzy with pleasure, he dared more.

Her eyes widened.

He started to ease back, but she clamped onto his bottom with both hands.

"Keep going," she begged. "Oh, Boone, please keep going."

"Shelby, I'm afraid I'll—" *Lose control. Love you too much to ever let go.*

"Keep going," she begged, her breath coming in quick gasps. "Oh, please."

As he sank further, her body opened to him in a way that he'd never known, hadn't even imagined was possible. She was inviting him into her soul.

Then he felt her first contractions. With a groan of complete surrender he slid deep as they both came wildly undone. He captured her cries against his mouth as they held on tight and rode the whirlwind, locked completely and irretrievably...together.

15

As the waves of Shelby's powerful climax receded, the tears came. She couldn't have held them back if she'd wanted to.

Instantly Boone tensed. "I hurt you."

"No," she choked out, still sobbing. "Just hold me. I need you to hold me."

He cradled her gently, absorbing the torrent without protest or judgment. While he remained solidly within her, as if anchoring her to his strength, she wept in his arms.

She cried for the ugliness she'd endured and she cried for the beauty he'd given her. Months of silent suffering poured out, feelings for which she had no words, sorrows she'd buried deep. He'd uncovered it all.

At last she hiccupped to a stop, exhausted, but feeling a hundred pounds lighter, free of grief she'd bottled up for a long time. Her nose was stuffed up and no doubt her eyes were red.

She gazed up into his beloved face and knew from his tender expression that no apology was necessary. They didn't need to talk it out, or analyze why she'd cried. He knew. She didn't even feel embarrassed about the way she must look, because she knew he didn't care.

Because he loved her. She knew it as surely as she knew the sun would rise. He didn't need to say it. The truth was in his soft green eyes.

"Lie still," he murmured easing away from her. "I'll get some tissues so you can blow your nose."

She missed him the instant he withdrew and levered his warm body out of the bed. As if he knew that, too, he pulled the comforter over her before he left the room. But a comforter would never substitute for his strong arms. And without him deep inside her, she felt hollow. She wanted him back with her, surrounding her, entering her, being one with her.

No doubt about it, he was immense. She might be a little sore tomorrow, as if that mattered. Given time, her body would adjust to his size. Time—that might be the one thing she would never be given.

He came back into the room—six feet, five inches of the most breathtaking body she'd ever seen. There was much to admire about this man, yet her attention went unerringly to his groin. Even at rest, his male equipment was impressive.

But as he stepped into the light and held out the box of tissues, she noticed the big angry bruise on his shoulder. "You *are* hurt."

He smiled. "Can't feel a thing."

She sat up and the comforter fell away from her breasts. "You should do something for that." She took a tissue and blew her nose. "Ice or something."

"It's probably too late for ice." His gaze lingered on her breasts.

"Then first-aid cream." She noticed the direction of his gaze. She also noticed the twitch of his penis. Her body answered with a quickening of its own, but she was concerned about his shoulder. The bruise was a rainbow of colors. It looked nasty. "There must be something to take the pain away."

"There is." His eyes grew hot as he reached for the comforter.

MUCH LATER, Shelby fell asleep in Boone's arms. The day-bed was a tight fit for the two of them, which was exactly how Shelby liked it. Boone seemed quite happy with the arrangement, too, as he turned off the light and wrapped himself protectively around her.

When he cupped her breast and pressed his groin against her bottom, she remembered his embarrassment waking up in the New Mexico motel room in exactly this position. This time, she thought as she drifted to sleep, he wouldn't need to be embarrassed when he woke up with an erection. In fact, she quite looked forward to it.

She awoke to darkness and movement as Boone eased out of bed. Turning over, she saw him pulling on his jeans. She whispered his name.

He leaned down and kissed her. "I heard something. Probably Josh getting up to go potty. I'll go check on him, make sure he didn't pee in the closet. Keep the bed warm."

It probably was Josh, she told herself. Yet something didn't feel right to her. And maybe Josh would need her. As Boone started toward the door, she leaned down and picked up her panties and shirt. She'd slip them on, just in case Boone needed her help with Josh.

Not that Boone needed her help, she thought as she pulled on the underwear and pushed her arms into the shirtsleeves. Josh idolized Boone and would do anything the man asked of him.

Boone stepped into the hallway. "Josh?" he called softly. "What's going on, buddy?"

She had three buttons fastened when she heard Boone fall, hitting the floor in the hallway with enough force to shake the floorboards.

"Boone?" Oh, God, he'd tripped over something. Josh must have left a toy truck in the hall, although she thought they'd picked up everyth—

"Shebby! Shebby, help!"

Her blood ran cold. Something was very wrong. "Josh! I'm coming!"

She barreled into the hall and saw Boone lying motionless, his huge body nearly filling the narrow hall. She fought nausea.

"Shebby! Help me!"

"Shut up, you little monster! I'm your father, and you're coming with me!"

Mason. The blood roared in her ears.

"No! You hurt Boone!" Josh screamed. "You hurt my Boone! Shebby!"

She didn't stop to check on Boone. Mason had Josh. *But why weren't the dogs tearing him apart?* As Elizabeth started wailing, Shelby jumped over Boone and ran into the darkened bedroom.

Inside she faced her worst nightmare. Mason had an arm around Josh's middle while the little boy flailed and kicked at him.

"You hurt Boone!" he screamed. "You hurt my Boone!"

The dogs stood looking from the hysterical baby in the crib to the man and boy struggling next to the bed. They seemed bewildered and sluggish. The facts hit Shelby like bullets. *Mason had found a way to drug the dogs. He'd knocked Boone unconscious or...* No. Her mind couldn't go there.

But for now, she was the only one left to stop him.

A sense of calm resolution came over her. If Mason planned to take that boy out of this house, he would have to kill her first. "Put him down, Mason."

"Not in this lifetime," Mason said with a sneer. "I'm taking him and walking out of this house." He took a step toward her. "Get outta my way, bitch."

As her eyes adjusted to the dim light she could see that he wore camouflage gear and his eyes glittered with an unholy fire. She looked for his weapon and saw some sort of billy club hanging from his belt. No gun. He was probably smart enough to know taking Josh at gunpoint wouldn't look good to the courts. And he was arrogant enough about his physical abilities that he thought he wouldn't need a gun for this job. He probably saw himself as on the kind of mission he imagined when he'd tried so hard to become a SEAL.

She reached behind her for the door handle and flung the door shut. Then she backed against it and turned the lock. "I'm not moving. Put him down."

"You're a joke. I could squash you like a fly."

"Don't hurt my Shebby!" Josh screamed, and he began to cry.

"Shut *up*, I said! Or I'll give you something to cry about!"

Shelby stepped forward, her rage solidifying into cold hate. "You so much as leave a mark on Josh and you'll never get custody, Mason."

He glared at her. "I can sure as hell leave a mark on you. Most judges would understand if I went a little crazy trying to get my precious son back from the crazy woman who snatched him. So stand back and let me pass."

"No." She flexed her knees and tried to remember what she'd learned in her self-defense course. She seemed pitifully inadequate for the job.

Josh, however, was not. He grabbed Mason's hand and bit him.

Mason yelled in surprise and dropped Josh to the floor. "Son of a bitch!" He drew back his foot as if to kick the little boy.

With a cry of fury Shelby launched herself at him, and to her surprise she knocked him backward onto the bed. The image of his foot drawn back ready to kick Josh brought out primitive instincts she'd never felt before. Lessons in self-defense disappeared in a red haze as she kicked, scratched and clawed. She wanted to kill him.

But she was losing the fight. He grabbed her wrists and shoved her backwards, following her down to the floor with a snarl. Straddling her, he released one of her wrists long enough to backhand her across the face. She saw stars. Then his thumbs closed over her windpipe.

"Stop, stop, stop!" screeched Josh, flailing at Mason.

Shelby caught a glimpse of gold in Josh's hand. He'd picked up his precious stone and was trying to hit his father with it, which might enrage Mason even more. While she struggled to pull Mason's hands away, she tried to tell Josh to stay back, but Mason was choking off her wind.

Josh's aim was bad and his strength puny, but he managed to connect with Mason's ear.

With a yelp of pain, Mason loosened his grip on Shelby's throat, clutched his bleeding ear and twisted toward Josh. "I'll kill you for that, you little runt!"

Desperately Shelby lunged for his face to bring his attention back to her. She succeeded.

"Right after I take care of you, bitch," he said, breathing hard.

"If you kill either of us," she rasped, "you'll never get that money."

"Shut up." He smacked her across the mouth and she tasted blood. "And you're wrong. I have a new plan. I'm gonna burn this place down, all of you in it. So sad. Shouldn't leave live ashes in the fireplace, you know. And guess what? I'm the kid's only surviving parent." His fingers closed around her throat. "Don't worry. I'll get the money. Why do you think I rigged up that little boating *accident*?"

He'd killed her parents and sister. Filled with horror, she fought him as best she could, but her strength was going. The sounds of Josh yelling and Elizabeth crying faded as Mason choked off her air supply. A giant vise seemed to be squeezing her chest. A loud crash sounded somewhere in the distance, but she couldn't make sense of it.

Then came a roar, as if from some enraged beast, and Mason was lifted high in the air. As she struggled to draw breath into her burning lungs she heard furniture splinter. Summoning all her will, she rolled to one side and looked for Josh. She finally saw him. He'd climbed in the crib with Elizabeth and wrapped his arms around her, but she was still crying. Both dogs were cowering under the crib.

Shelby crawled to the crib, put an arm through the slats and wrapped it around Josh. His small body quivered with terror.

"It's okay," she whispered automatically. She didn't know if it was okay or not. The two men fought like animals only a few feet away. She couldn't tell who was winning.

"It's okay," he whispered back, his voice shaking. "Boone gots him."

Sure enough, Boone had the upper hand at last. He held Mason down and his free arm worked like a piston as he pummeled the other man unmercifully.

Shelby remembered how she'd felt when Mason had threatened Josh, and she knew if she didn't do something, Boone wouldn't stop until Mason was dead. She gave Josh a squeeze. "Stay here."

"You, too!"

"No. I have to go. I'll be okay." She crawled closer to the men and tried to make her vocal chords work. "*Boone!*" she cried, but only a squawk came out. She moved even closer, cringing at the crunch of bone against bone as Boone hit Mason again and again.

"Boone!" she squawked again. "Boone, stop! Boone, please stop!"

No response. He seemed oblivious to everything but the task of eliminating Mason Fowler from the face of the earth.

She swallowed and tried again. "If you love me, stop!"

His head came up. His eyes held the wild spark of a predator as he gazed at her, and there was no recognition, as if he couldn't remember who she was. Mason lay unconscious beneath him, his face bloody. But he was still breathing.

"Boone, I love you," she rasped. "Don't kill him. You'll go to jail. We can't be together if you go to jail."

Slowly the killing rage faded from his eyes. He glanced down at Mason.

"He's not going anywhere," Shelby said.

"Josh?" Boone murmured.

"He's okay." She turned toward the crib. "He's taking care of Elizabeth."

Boone looked over at the crib. Then his gaze came back to rest on Shelby's face. He looked disoriented as he reached out a hand and lightly touched her cheek.

Even that gentle touch hurt, but she forced herself not to wince. "I'm fine."

Slowly she stood and held out her hand. "Come on," she said, her voice still hoarse. "Let's get the kids and go call the police."

He put his hand in hers and got to his feet. They walked hand in hand over to the crib. She lifted Elizabeth out and he picked up Josh. But he didn't move. Instead he stood there, as if in shock, while he held tight to Josh and gazed at Shelby and Elizabeth.

Josh looked up into Boone's stricken face and stroked his cheek. "Let's cuddle," he murmured.

With a broken sob Boone reached out and gathered Shelby and Elizabeth into his embrace.

Two HOURS LATER, the police and the paramedics had come and gone. Fowler was in custody. Boone had given a brief statement telling the officers what he'd heard before he'd broken down the bedroom door. Good thing Fowler had admitted he'd arranged the accident that had killed Shelby's parents, and Boone had regained consciousness in time to hear it. Fowler's chances of getting custody of Josh were finished.

Boone had gathered his charges in the living room by a roaring fire, unable to think of putting Josh or Elizabeth back into the bedroom after what had just happened there. Josh had insisted they all deserved gold stars, so Shelby had dutifully pasted one on each of them. She'd put Elizabeth's on the back of her sleeper so she wouldn't be able to pull it off and eat it.

Josh dozed on the sofa clutching his blankie, and Elizabeth lay asleep in her playpen nearby, her monkey Bruce clutched in one tiny fist. Boone sat on the braided rug with Shelby tucked between his outstretched legs, her back propped against his chest. He knew she wasn't asleep.

Boone supposed the night wasn't really cold enough for a fire, but he was. Every time he thought of Fowler's hands on Shelby's throat he turned to ice inside. He would have killed the bastard if she hadn't stopped him.

As he cradled her in front of the fire he thought of the words she'd used to penetrate his murderous rage. *I love you.*

He'd been thinking about those words ever since the patrol car had pulled away from the house about a half hour ago. They'd run through his head as he and Shelby had hauled Josh and Elizabeth's stuff out to the living room and tucked the kids into bed next to the fire.

Although he and Shelby had talked to Josh and Elizabeth as they'd sung songs and played little games to make things seem okay again, they hadn't talked to each other. After the kids were settled, he'd pulled Shelby down and drawn her up against him. She'd come willingly, but she was very, very quiet.

Boone had to face the fact that everything was changed. So much had happened in only a few hours. First he'd discovered how much he loved Shelby when she'd cried in his arms, and he'd wondered how the hell he'd live without her if Jessica demanded marriage. And then he'd seen Shelby's life nearly snuffed out before his eyes, and he'd realized he couldn't live without her, period.

He had to be with her, see her every morning and sleep next to her every night. His world wouldn't turn unless she was in it. His duty might be to Jessica, and maybe he was supposed to pay for his mistake in getting her pregnant, but he loved Shelby more than duty, and he'd find another way to pay for his mistake.

He took a deep breath and wrapped his arms tighter around Shelby. "Marry me," he said.

She didn't answer for a very long time. Finally she spoke, and she sounded suspiciously close to tears. "Do you mean that?"

"I've never meant anything more in my life."

She scooted around so she could see his face, and sure enough, tears welled in her eyes. Her voice was choked. "I thought you wanted to find out about Jessica, about Elizabeth. I thought everything depended on that."

"It did." He framed her face in his big hands. Every time he looked at the bruise on her cheek and the cut on her lip, his insides twisted. "Until I almost lost you forever. I can't lose you, Shelby." He felt tears burning at the backs of his eyes, too. "I just can't."

She swallowed. "I don't want to lose you, either, Boone."

"I'm no good at fancy speeches." His chest felt tight, full of emotions he didn't know how to explain. "I wish I was.

You deserve that. I only know I have to be with you, Shelby. There's no other way."

"I don't need fancy speeches." She reached up and touched his cheek. "Just three little words."

He let out a long, shuddering breath. He knew those words. "I love you." His voice almost broke as he said them. He'd almost lost the chance to tell her.

"Those would be the words." Her eyes glowed as she gazed up at him. "The only ones either of us will ever need." She drew closer, her sweet breath warm on his face. "I love you," she whispered.

The joy that surged through him began to ease the cold chill that had surrounded his heart. He touched her mouth with the tip of his finger. "I want to kiss you, but I don't want to hurt your mouth," he murmured.

"Kiss me," she said, brushing her mouth against his, "and make it better."

He kissed her gently, but she responded with such heat that he nearly forgot to be careful. No telling what might have happened if Josh's childish voice hadn't interrupted them.

"You're *kissing!*" he said.

Boone turned to look at Josh. "Is that okay with you?"

Josh sat up and rubbed at his eyes. "I guess so, but you gots to get married now. Like Travis and Gwen. They kissed in front of all the peoples, and now, bam, they're married."

Boone sighed and glanced at Shelby. "You heard him. I guess we have to."

Her eyes sparkled. "Well, if we have to, we have to."

Boone turned back to Josh. "How would you like that, if Shelby and I got married?"

"Oh, I would," Josh said sleepily, flopping back down.

"Glad to hear it," Boone said with a chuckle.

Josh yawned. "And y'know what?"
"What?"
Josh snuggled into his pillow and closed his eyes. "Bob, he would like it, too."

Epilogue

SEVEN ADULTS, a three-year-old boy and a five-month-old baby girl strained the resources of Doc Harrison's waiting room, especially when none of them seemed inclined to stay still. Shelby decided to concentrate on making sure Josh behaved himself.

"Maybe somebody should go outside and wait there until the doc is ready to see us." Sebastian, who was holding baby Elizabeth, glared pointedly at Travis and Boone.

"Not likely." Travis put an arm around Gwen. "We're all in this together, and nobody's going to hear about this paternity test before anybody else."

Josh stopped running his truck over the floor and looked up. "What's a 'ternity test?"

"That's the doctor's test I told you about." Shelby crouched down next to him. "To find out once and for all who's Elizabeth's father."

"My daddy's in jail. He's sick in the head." Josh spoke the fact as if announcing the time of day before going back to his truck race.

Shelby glanced up at Boone. He gazed down at her, offering silent support. They'd decided not to sugarcoat the truth about Mason in some attempt to spare Josh. Fortunately Josh had never formed a real bond with his biological father. Boone was quickly becoming the most important man in his life.

Two weeks had passed since that traumatic night when Mason had broken into the ranch house. Some days Shelby felt impatient that everything hadn't been finalized, but the wedding date was set and the custody hearing scheduled soon afterward. Following that, she and Boone would set the wheels in motion for adoption.

It was just details, paperwork and red tape, she told herself. In all ways that mattered they were already a family. They'd even talked to Sebastian about buying Matty's house and some acreage around it.

Only the question of Elizabeth remained unanswered. With still no word from Jessica, the men had decided to take the step they'd been avoiding and settle the matter medically. The atmosphere in Doc Harrison's waiting room was tense.

"The point I'm trying to make," Sebastian persisted, "is that all these bodies are making it too hot in here for Elizabeth."

"It's how you're holding her," Travis said. "Lizzy prefers a looser grip. And you might try playing peekaboo with her or something. You're such an old sobersides this morning, no wonder she's fussy. Better yet, let me have her."

"No, I'll take her, now." Boone stepped toward Sebastian. "I'm the tallest, so I can hold her up high, where the air's better. And cooler."

Luann Evans edged over toward Sebastian. "Heat rises," she said. "So you'd better give that precious bundle to me. Grandmothers know a few things about tending to a fussy little girl, don't we, sweetheart?"

Sebastian stepped away from the crowd. "She's fine where she is. Besides, it's my turn. Everybody else has already had her."

"Yeah, but you've had her the longest," Travis grumbled. "Fair is fair, right, Boone?"

Matty rolled her eyes. "I have a watch with a second

hand. We could time the baby rotation like a bronc-riding event if it would make you three cowboys happier."

"I'm a cowboy, too!" Josh said happily. "I gots a hat, and I gots boots."

"And they look great," Shelby said.

"Yep. I wanna go ride horsies."

"Sounds good to me, too," Travis said. "I hate this waiting. What's the doc doing in there so long with Nellie, giving her a hip replacement?"

Gwen laid a hand on his arm. "You wouldn't want him to rush his appointment with Nellie."

"Hell if I wouldn't." Travis gave her a rebellious stare. When she frowned at him, he grinned sheepishly. "Just this one time."

"I wouldn't mind if he skipped the bedside manner this morning, myself," Sebastian said. "I mean, I know she's getting up in years, but—"

The examining room door opened and Nellie Coogan shuffled out. She paused to peer through her thick glasses at the crowd in the waiting room.

Shelby stood and walked over to slip her hand inside Boone's. The moment had come. Boone clutched her hand like a lifeline.

"Hey, there, Miz Coogan," Travis said, touching the brim of his hat. "I hope you're in good health on this fine morning."

A chorus of greetings and good wishes followed as everyone else in the room remembered their manners.

"Thank you." Nellie continued to study them with obvious curiosity. Finally she nodded to herself. "I always wondered what they meant by those group health plans. This must be what those folks on the TV are talking about. How smart of you all." Then she shuffled out the door.

Nobody bothered to watch her leave as they turned toward the examining room door where a small, bearded man in a white coat stood quietly.

The silence lengthened.

Finally Sebastian spoke, his voice shaking. "You might as well spit it out, Doc. Which one of us is this baby's father?"

Doc Harrison cleared his throat. "I went over the results several times, because I wanted to make sure. The fact is, gentlemen..."

"Aw, come on, Doc," Travis said. "Don't drag it out."

"Yeah," Boone added. "Just say it. Which one?"

The small doctor adjusted his glasses. "None of you."

Who is little Elizabeth's real daddy?
And what kind of trouble could Jessica
possibly be running from that she'd have to
abandon her baby?

For the answer to these questions
and more, watch for

THAT'S MY BABY!

a single title release
available September 2000.

Here's a preview!

1

JESSICA FRANKLIN'S stomach gurgled with anxiety as she waited at JFK for the 5:45 flight from London. After seventeen months apart, she had to meet Nat Grady, the man she'd loved—still loved, damn it—disguised as a bag lady. Then she had to tell him about Elizabeth, the baby he had no idea they'd conceived, the baby she'd left in Colorado to keep her safe.

The embarrassing truth was, Jessica had picked up a stalker. She thought of it like that, as if she'd contracted a deadly disease and was no longer fit to be a mother. Growing up, she felt stifled by her wealthy father's attempts to protect her from kidnappers. She'd left home, spurning a life of bulletproof cars and bodyguards, insisting she could live quietly and anonymously without all that. It infuriated her to be wrong.

About ten feet away, a woman clucked and cooed at the baby in her arms. Jessica ached every time she saw a mother and baby. For her own good she shouldn't watch them, but she couldn't seem to stop torturing herself. Babies drew her like magnets. When she spotted one she'd stare shamelessly as she tried to guess the child's age and wonder whether Elizabeth would look anything like that, act anything like that.

This one could be around eight months old, Elizabeth's age, and was a boy, judging from the outfit. Jessica couldn't imagine her baby this size. When she'd left her at the Rocking D Ranch, Elizabeth had been so tiny, just barely two months old. Jessica had never imagined that their separation would be this long. But now that Nat was home, she would see her baby again. Soon.

The little boy laughed and Jessica counted four teeth. Elizabeth would have teeth by now. She would be crawling, getting into everything, learning to make noises that were the beginnings of speech.

Like ma-ma.

Jessica endured the pain. At least Elizabeth was safe. She'd known she could count on Sebastian, Travis and Boone to keep her that way until Nat came home and they could all decide what to do.

Weary passengers trudged into the gate area from customs and Jessica's pulse raced as she anticipated the meeting to come. She still hadn't decided on her approach. The thought of Nat Grady brought up so many emotions she had to ask them to stand in line and take turns being heard.

Usually the first emotion to shoulder its way to the front was anger. She'd fallen head-over-heels in love with the guy, but for the year they'd been involved he'd insisted they keep their relationship secret from everyone but his secretary Bonnie, a woman who had invented the word discreet. Even his best friends, the three men she'd left in charge of Elizabeth, didn't know she and Nat had been seeing each other.

She should have recognized the secrecy thing as a warning signal, but love was blind, and she'd accepted his explanation that his friends were a nosy bunch and he didn't want outside interference in their relationship until they knew where it was going. All the while Nat had jolly well known where it was going, she thought bitterly. On a train bound for nowhere.

If only she could hate him for that. God, how she'd tried.

Instead she kept thinking of what he'd said the night they'd broken up. *I shouldn't have let you waste your time on me. I'm not worth it.*

Then he'd left her, his real-estate business and his friends to head for a tiny, war-torn country where he'd worked as a volunteer in the refugee camps. Along with her other emotions connected to Nat, Jessica battled guilt. If she hadn't pushed him to end the secrecy and marry her, he wouldn't have left the country. She was sure of it. He'd have stayed in Colorado, making love to her, the sweetest love she'd ever known.

Instead, to get away from her and the demons she'd demanded that he face, he'd stepped into a violent world where the lines of battle blurred and changed every day. As a civilian he had no weapons and no military training to protect him. He'd spent seventeen months in danger on account of her, and if he'd been killed or hurt, she would have blamed herself.

She was also to blame for the baby, after he'd told her flat out he never wanted kids. A woman her age should have known antibiotics jeopardized the effectiveness of birth control pills. But she had some gaps in her sexual education, thanks to growing up shadowed by her own personal bodyguard. She hadn't known.

She needed to tell him it was her responsibility. Still, she thought he should know about the baby, in case the stalker got lucky. But before she told him anything, she'd have to convince him who she was. The dark wig, the baggy clothes and the thick glasses wouldn't look familiar to him. But once he'd figured out who she was, what would she say first?

Nat, we have a baby girl named Elizabeth. Too abrupt. A man who'd said he never wanted children might need to be eased into that kind of discussion. *Nat, I'm disguised like this because I have a stalker on my trail*. Too scary. He'd just returned from dodging bullets. He deserved a little peace and quiet before she gave him that bad news, coupled with the information that if anything happened to her, he'd need to watch out for Elizabeth, whether he cared to or not.

Her stomach felt as if she'd swallowed a bag full of hot marbles.

A man in a business suit came toward the woman with the baby, and the baby bounced happily, reaching out for his daddy. When the father lifted the baby into his arms and showered him with kisses, Jessica had to look away.

She brushed the tears from her eyes. She had to pay attention. Nat could be coming along any minute, and she didn't want to miss him.

A tall man with a full beard and hair past his collar appeared in the stream of passengers. He wore a battered-looking leather jacket, jeans and boots. A scuffed backpack hung from one broad shoulder, a backpack not too different from the one she carried. Her gaze swept past him, then returned. He moved through the crowd with a familiar, fluid walk, as if he were striding along to a country tune. Nat walked that way.

She looked closer, past the rich brown of his beard, and her heart hammered. The mouth. She'd spent hours gazing at that chiseled mouth, classic as the mouth on one of her father's prized Rodin sculptures. She'd spent even more hours kissing and being kissed by that mouth, and her tongue slid over her lips in remembrance. Nat. In spite of the anger and guilt, pure joy bloomed within her at the sight of him. Nat. He was here. He was okay.

Suddenly whatever she decided to say seemed unimportant. She just had to get to him, wrap her arms around him and give thanks that he'd returned in one piece. Her nightmares had begun the day she'd learned where he was, and CNN had been her lifeline ever since.

No matter how furiously she'd counseled herself to remain neutral when she saw him, she was miles beyond that. She was weepy with gratitude for his safe return. He was an oasis in the desert her life had become without him.

Drinking in the sight of him moving through the crowd, she sighed with happiness. Thank God he looked healthy, his skin tanned and his hair still lustrous, reflecting the terminal's overhead lights. But she'd give him the herbal supplements she'd brought, anyway, and insist that he take them. He didn't eat right under the best of circumstances, and no telling what he'd existed on over there.

He was so appealing that she couldn't help wondering if he'd become involved with anyone while he was gone. A beautiful waif of a woman, perhaps, who spoke little English, but who had awakened his protective instincts. A woman who'd fallen deeply in love with the big, handsome American cowboy who'd come to help. Jessica knew how easily such a thing could happen, and her heart hurt.

But if he had found another love, that wasn't her business. He was free to do as he chose.

Seventeen months. That was a long time for a single man of thirty-three to go without sex. He might not have fallen in love, but he might have taken a woman to bed....

She wouldn't ask. No, she definitely wouldn't ask. But the thought made her want to cry.

Moving closer, she focused on his face, trying to meet his gaze. They'd had a magic connection between them, and maybe if she caught his eye, he'd see beyond her disguise and recognize her, heart-to-heart. He'd be startled, of course, and might wonder if she'd gone crazy while he was out of the country.

In a way she had. Crazy with worry...and love. Still love.

But she wouldn't let him know that she still loved him. She would be very careful about that, unless...unless he had gone a little crazy, too. Although she'd lectured herself to squash that hope like a bug, she'd let it live.

At last Nat glanced her way, and she opened her mouth to call to him. But instead of calling his name, she drew back in uncertainty. His gaze was so hard and uncompromising that it intimidated her. He'd changed.

If you enjoyed what you just read,
then we've got an offer you can't resist!

Take 2 bestselling
love stories FREE!
Plus get a FREE surprise gift!

HARLEQUIN®
Temptation

COMING NEXT MONTH

#789 FOR HER EYES ONLY Tori Carrington
The Magnificent McCoy Men

Immigration agent Jake McCoy prided himself on being a loner.
So how had illegal alien Michelle Lambert stolen her way into
his heart—and his bed—so quickly? The gorgeous French
woman was searching for her young daughter and refused to go
home without her. So, torn between desire and duty, what else
could Jake do but marry her?

#790 MORGAN Lori Foster
The Buckhorn Brothers, Bk. 2

Morgan Hudson commanded a lot of respect as Buckhorn's
biggest, baddest sheriff. How one sexy little city woman could
turn him on his head was a mystery, not to mention downright
aggravating! But Misty Malone did just that, and Morgan
couldn't wait to get rid of her…until he discovered why she'd
shown up in the first place.

#791 SHAMELESS Kimberly Raye
Blaze

The last thing Deb Strickland wanted was a man—especially
one like hunky Jimmy Mission. But when faced with Jimmy's
killer-cowboy charm, Deb couldn't help reacting—even if it was
by slamming into his truck! She thought having to pay damages
was bad…until Jimmy came up with a solution that was
absolutely *shameless….*

#792 SEDUCTIVELY YOURS Gina Wilkins
The Wild McBrides, Bk. 2

Jamie Flaherty had always been in love with sexy-as-sin
Trevor McBride. And now that he'd been chased home by
scandal, she wasn't waiting any longer. Only, Trevor didn't need
any more notoriety…and his relationship with Jamie, the girl
from the wrong side of the tracks, was sure to encourage even
more gossip. But he didn't stand a chance once Jamie decided to
seduce him….

CNM0600